Acts of Resistance

by Dominic Carrillo

SANTA
MONICA
PRESS
TEEN

Published by:
Santa Monica Press LLC
P.O. Box 850
Solana Beach, CA 92075
1-800-784-9553
www.santamonicapress.com
books@santamonicapress.com

Printed in the United States

Santa Monica Press books are available at special quantity discounts when purchased in bulk by corporations, organizations, or groups. Please call our Special Sales department at 1-800-784-9553.

ISBN-13 978-1-59580-119-7

Publisher's Cataloging-in-Publication data
Names: Carrillo, Dominic, author.
Title: Acts of resistance / by Dominic Carrillo.
Description: Solana Beach, CA: Santa Monica Press, 2023.
Identifiers: ISBN: 978-1-59580-119-7 (paperback) | 978-1-59580-770-0 (ebook)
Subjects: LCSH Jews--Bulgaria--History--Fiction. | World War, 1939-1945--Jews--Rescue--Bulgaria--Fiction. | Bulgaria--History--1941-1944--Fiction. | Bulgaria--Ethnic relations--Fiction. | Historical fiction. | BISAC YOUNG ADULT FICTION / Historical / Holocaust | YOUNG ADULT FICTION / Historical / Military & Wars | YOUNG ADULT FICTION / People & Places / Europe | YOUNG ADULT FICTION / Religious / Jewish
Classification: LCC PS3603 .A77 A38 2023 | DDC 813.6--dc23

Cover and interior design and production by Future Studio
Cover image of woman courtesy of www.Figurestock.com / Paul Thomas Gooney; background: Tryfonov

For Ella

Uncovered in the Bulgarian National Archives, the following three narratives are based on memoirs written soon after World War II.

These documents were hidden during the communist era (1945–1989) because they did not align with party propaganda, which claimed that communist resistance groups during the war were the only ones who saved approximately 48,000 Bulgarian Jews from the Holocaust.

The true story of a few brave politicians, church officials, and, above all, ordinary people—who stood up against the government, fought for what was right, and made a significant difference—was the last thing the communist regime wanted the population to know.

I

LILY

The year I graduated high school, we entered the war on the side of Nazi Germany.

The year after that, I landed what my friends and family considered to be a great job in the capital, working for the Bulgarian government as Alexander Belev's personal secretary. Belev was in charge of a new department called the Komisarstvo za Evreiskite Vuprosi (Commissariat for Jewish Questions), but we never called it that. We always called it KEV, and everyone who worked there knew our main task was to institute the recently passed "Laws for the Defense of the Nation." We didn't see them as anti-Jewish laws back then because we'd been convinced that our patriotic duty—not to mention our salaried job—was to keep Bulgaria safe from any threat to the war effort. Our office put into place important security measures concerning only "threatening" members of the Jewish community, and that was it.

So I thought.

Everything changed on March 5, 1943, when Belev brought me to the train station in Skopje, Macedonia.

That's where I first witnessed my dull paperwork being put into horrendous action.

That's where I watched men being beaten and dragged by soldiers. That's where I heard mothers screaming and children wailing, as they were forced onto cattle cars.

But I most vividly remember the blank, silent stare of a pale, dark-haired woman who must have been utterly terrified by her sudden lack of control. Her infant baby cried in her arms, wrapped in a gray woolen blanket. As a pimply-faced soldier prodded her toward the train, the woman looked at me again as if she could see through me—as if she knew I had a hand in this whole wretched scene. Her baby screamed as a soldier pushed her up the ramp with the butt of his rifle, into the train car and out of sight. The pale woman and her child were only two souls in a procession of thousands.

Thousands who were no longer numbers on a page.

They were real individuals whose lives were being torn apart before my eyes.

Standing next to my boss, a single tear fell down my cheek.

"Not what you expected?" Mr. Belev asked me.

I couldn't respond.

What I was witnessing was the forced deportation of Macedonian Jews from Bulgarian-held territory to forced-labor camps—11,343 men, women, and children, to be exact. I knew the precise number because I had typed the official deportation document for Belev myself.

That day in Skopje changed everything for me.

MARCH 6, 1943

PETER

Holding it in both hands, I stared at David's RAF Spitfire model airplane in disbelief. He hurried away to avoid shedding tears in front of me, his best friend.

I realized in that moment that David was my best friend.

I didn't even know he was Jewish until sixth grade, when he told me about Kristallnacht. But soon everyone knew about that stuff. Even as a kid, you didn't have to have a Jewish best friend to know about Adolf Hitler and the Nazis.

We also heard about a few forced evictions and round-ups of Jews in German-occupied territories, though that was not publicized. As a teenager in Bulgaria, I had only heard about these acts of war in other places in Europe. Back then it all seemed to be happening so far away.

It didn't affect me personally—and I didn't think it ever would—until my third year in high school. Sure, Bulgaria had officially sided with the Nazis earlier, but no evil plan to target Jews had surfaced yet. Yeah, curfews and property restrictions were officially placed on our small Jewish population, but nothing seemed to be enforced. Even the order to pin yellow stars on their sleeves was more joked about than respected by anyone—even the local police. After all, the Jewish community in my hometown could hardly be considered a threat. For me, anti-Semitism was especially ridiculous. I'd been playing football in the streets with my neighbor David since I was a little kid. I ate dinner with his family sometimes. They were always kind to me. Our parents were good friends.

All of my innocence—or ignorance—about being safe and distanced from the war came crashing down on the morning of March 6, 1943, when we heard the news.

The previous day, four of David's relatives had been forced from their homes, stripped of their belongings, and packed onto trains in nearby Macedonia. All their property was stolen by the soldiers.

They took thousands of them. Families were separated—husbands from wives, mothers from children. Some resisters were brutally beaten by police.

The rumor was that Bulgarian cities were next.

We knew *our town* was next.

Soldiers had recently been seen in Kyustendil clearing out an old tobacco warehouse right next to the train tracks on the edge of town. Taken with the recent news from Skopje, the purpose of those warehouses became frighteningly clear.

By noon of the same day, David and his family were already trying to liquidate their furniture, clothes, and valuables before it was all taken away, even though the sale of personal property had just been made illegal for Jews. Everything turned frantic very quickly.

David's hands trembled as he handed me his prized model Spitfire (his dream was to become a pilot). Though we were nearly grown up at seventeen, we were both very familiar with each others' childhood toys, hobbies, and dreams.

"What are you doing?" I asked.

"I'm giving this to you so the soldiers don't destroy it."

"What? This is your best plane. I can't."

"My father said they'll deport us because we're Jewish. They'll take everything."

"That's not gonna happen," I said. "Not here."

He looked at me solemnly, tears welling in his eyes.

"Peter," he said. "It's already happening."

As David walked back to his house that day, I made a vow: I wouldn't let any Nazis take away my best friend, or his family.

No matter what.

MISHO

Stopped at a railroad crossing near Dupnitsa, I sat behind the wheel of a car with one very important passenger. It was uncomfortable—not solely because I'd had my license for only one month, but because I was technically in hiding while chauffeuring the most prominent archbishop in the country, Metropolitan Stefan. A nice man, but very eccentric, he sometimes went long spans without saying a word.

In this case, we had ridden in silence for almost an hour.

However, it wasn't my serious lack of driving experience—or my hidden identity, or the awkwardly silent national figure in the back seat—that made me remember our stop at the railroad crossing that day.

The train passed in front of us, going very slowly, and I saw people's hands and arms reaching out of the slits of the cattle cars. They were yelling to us for help in many different languages—Bulgarian, Greek, Hebrew.

Normal time stopped.

It didn't seem real.

When I turned to ask Stefan what was going on, the back seat was empty.

The archbishop, already outside of the car, had his arms extended toward the passing train, as if he could reach the outstretched hands and pull them out with the help of God. But the train kept rolling, each metallic click a grim reminder of our powerlessness against this relentless machine. Pained human voices rang out, until the surreal procession had passed.

"Misho!" Stefan yelled. "Get us back to Sofia as quickly as you can." The archbishop jumped into the back seat faster than I'd ever seen him move. "Let's go!"

I had no idea what was going on.

LILY

On the train back from Skopje to Sofia, I couldn't help but feel guilty.

Not only was I sitting in a comfortable seat with all of my belongings and dignity intact, but I was also next to Alexander Belev, the man who was primarily responsible for rounding up over 10,000 people and packing them onto trains like livestock.

Glancing over at his sharp, sinister jawline, I envisioned the paperwork crossing my desk that had reported the deportation of thousands of Jews from the region of Thrace—the part of northern Greece that Bulgaria had acquired, along with the Macedonian region of Yugoslavia, thanks to the Nazis. It was all part of the deal that put Bulgaria on Hitler's side.

"The Jews from Thrace," I said. "Were they . . . ?"

"Quarantined and deported too?" His voice was smug, proud. "Yes, yesterday and today."

Taken. Stolen. Robbed of everything.

"Eleven thousand, three hundred and forty-three of them in total?" I asked.

"Yes, indeed," Belev said, and smiled at me. "That's the exact number. You are a bright one."

Too used to being obedient, I ignored his condescension.

"Where are they all going?" I asked. "To Germany?"

"No," he said. "To Poland."

"To work at war munitions factories, I suppose?"

"I suppose they'll work," Belev said. "For a time."

For a time.

I knew what that meant. Though I had willfully ignored the meaning of the words, I'd seen pamphlets in the office that were titled "The Final Solution to the Jewish Problem." They included words like "eradicate" and "exterminate," as if these people were vermin to be disposed of. I didn't pay much attention because I considered it all to be war propaganda—only words used to rile people up, in an effort to unify the nation. The pamphlets didn't equate to people's lives, to families taken away, to children crying.

Until the train station in Skopje. *It is my fault, too.*

Outside my window, pine trees whizzed by. The branches still had tufts of snow on them. For at least a month, before the last melt and the arrival of spring, the world would be stark and monochromatic. No snow to cover up the leafless trees—only grays and browns—especially back in the city.

There was a brief time when I actually thought I liked Belev—a mature thirty-something lawyer with piercing eyes and a certain confidence about him. Now simply looking at him disgusted me.

"They'll be killed, won't they?" I asked.

Belev exhaled deeply from his mouth, but didn't answer me. He didn't have to.

"Will the same thing happen to the Jews in Sofia?"

"Lily, your questions are troubling," Belev mused.

He sniffed to keep his nose from running, rather than using a handkerchief. This added to my growing revulsion for him, but the pause made his line of thought weigh on me.

"You seem to be questioning the very basis of our work," he continued, "though in a surely *naive* way." He paused again, adding another layer of heaviness. "In case you've forgotten, Lily, our office must do one thing: protect the nation from those within who pose a threat to the war effort. We are in line with the Germans because they will win the war, and we will win back our pride and what is rightfully the land of Bulgaria."

He meant Thrace and Macedonia—what many Bulgarians considered *ours*, based on some old treaty and a brief period in history when it was part of "Greater Bulgaria."

"But—" I began.

He cut me off. "In order to win back our territory, as in any war, some blood must be shed," he explained to me, as if I were a child. "It's a fact of history. We can either be on the winning side or the losing side, but people will die regardless."

I tried to filter facts from Belev's bitter logic.

"Are you saying that the Jews who were sent away on the trains will die?"

"Yes, I am," he said, curtly. He looked out the window and combed his fingers through his pomaded hair. "Do you have a problem with this, Lily?"

"No," I said, almost automatically.

It was self-preservation—an instinct, I suppose. Though my heart sunk to the floor with the thought of those countless death sentences, I tried my best to hide it. I didn't want to lose my job at the beginning of my career. My parents back home in Stara Zagora depended on me to send them money every month. Now, after Skopje, it was undeniable that something was deeply wrong with my line of work, but I didn't want to be labeled a traitor—to be dismissed, even arrested. I wanted to do something, but I didn't know what. All I knew was that Belev needed to trust me, or I'd be fired right there in that train car.

"Sir, I understand what's best for Bulgaria," I said. "And I'm proud to protect our nation."

"Good," he said. "And it's best for Germany, too. *Heil Hitler!*"

"*Heil Hitler*," I said.

I'd repeated the two-word salute a few times before, but blindly—without thinking.

Now, for the first time, it meant something to me.

Something horrible.

For the rest of the ride back to Sofia, Belev's words echoed in my head: *We can either be on the winning side or the losing side, but people will die regardless.*

MISHO

The drive back to Sofia might have been absolutely silent if I hadn't spoken.

"Archbishop, what was happening back there . . . to the people on that train?"

No response.

Finally, he said gravely, "I can't believe it's actually happening."

No more than that.

I could guess what *it* was, but wasn't sure. He obviously didn't want to talk about *it*. Maybe he couldn't do so without breaking down. As we sped down the country road, a noxious lump formed in my throat at the mere thought of *it*.

Hitler's plan.

I glanced in the rearview mirror and saw Stefan signing the cross over and over, mumbling prayers.

Maybe a normal chauffeur would have left it at that and not bothered the elder clergyman, but I was curious—and far from a normal chauffeur.

"I heard some of those people pleading in Hebrew," I said.

"Me too," he whispered.

"Were they Jews?" I asked. "On that train."

"Yes, I believe so," Archbishop Stefan said.

"Where are they taking them?"

"I don't know, Misho, but they must be stopped."

"They're going to the camps?" I asked.

"Probably to the camps."

He didn't say *death camps* then, but he had the day we met.

Exactly one month before the cattle car sighting in Dupnitsa, I sat alone in Archbishop Stefan's house, in a modest living room that smelled of charred candles. When he walked in to meet me, he seemed unlike any man I'd ever seen. His dark, heavy robes and the thick chain bearing a silver crucifix immediately marked him as holy. But his discerning eyes and strong brow lent him a certain nobility. The long black beard below his overgrown mustache, almost completely gray, made him look like an aged lion—powerful yet serenely confident.

The archbishop sat down and looked as if he felt sorry for me. He didn't say a word.

It was awkward.

"Um, hello Archbishop Stefan." My words stumbled out. "Um, Your Majesty."

"Majesty?" he said. "You can't be serious."

"I'm sorry."

"*You're* sorry?" he said. "My name is Stefan. What do you have to be sorry about, kid?"

Am I still a kid? I'm eighteen years old.

I remained silent. Dumbstruck.

"Do you know why you're here?" Stefan asked.

My mother, an old friend of Stefan's, had told me that the archbishop was looking for a young man to work for him, though the job description was unclear. It seemed odd that an Orthodox Christian clergyman would want to employ a non-religious Jewish boy, but my mom wanted me to get a job and get out of the house. The problem was that I could not hold certain occupations under the new anti-Jewish laws.

I finally answered him.

"I'm here to get a job . . . I mean, unofficially."

The high priest stroked his beard for a while, let out an odd snort, then rested his hands on his big belly. Stefan was not short on idiosyncrasies.

"You are here," he said, "because you are in great danger, Michael."

Silence followed, making the archbishop's labored breathing more pronounced and foreboding.

"Danger? I thought my mom said—"

"Listen. Your mother cares deeply for you, which is why she sent you to me."

He readjusted his robes and leaned forward.

"The laws persecuting Jews are about to grow stronger, and the forces pushing for the extermination of your people are about to hit this country like never before."

"I don't get it. The Nazis are invading Bulgaria?"

"No," he said. "They're already here. And the Bulgarian collaborators who fear Hitler's wrath want to please him by carrying out his plans."

"And send us all to labor camps?" I asked.

"As far as I know, the Nazi plan is not to put all Jews to work in camps," the archbishop said gravely. "It's to take all Jews to *death* camps. The truth is that you are no longer safe with your family. Your mother and sister will go into hiding in a convent near Plovdiv. You will stay with me, work for me, but you will also be in hiding—protected behind the seminary walls."

"What?" I couldn't comprehend the massive, life-altering change.

"From this point on, you are no longer Michael, nor are you Jewish," he said. "Take off that little Star of David."

I hesitated, still confused about what was happening.

"Do it!" he said, then reached over and nearly ripped off the yellow star that was pinned to my front pocket. "From now on, your name is *Misho*. This nickname will help hide your identity, as will working for me. The assumption will be that you're just another Christian seminary student of mine."

I could have protested the swift stripping of my Jewish identity, but it was clearly too late for that. Like it or not, I had to quickly embrace survival mode.

"What about my mom?" I asked. "My sister?"

"They'll be fine, God willing. In good hands, in a convent far from the city."

Part of my soul deflated right there. I wasn't prepared for any of this.

"What am I going to do?"

My question was despairing and rhetorical, but Stefan took it as a practical one. He placed his pudgy hands on his knees before rising up and asking me, "Do you know how to drive an automobile, boy?"

"Yes," I said.

"Do you have a license?"

"No."

"Get one this week," he bellowed. "You'll be my driver, Misho, and I vow to protect you with God as my witness."

I didn't have much of a choice.

From that point on, I was Misho—the archbishop's chauffeur.

The rest of the drive back from Dupnitsa to Sofia was cold and silent.

The archbishop prayed, and I had time to think.

I pictured the train's steel wheels pushing forward

into the night. Those desperate hands and eyes grasping to escape the dark cattle cars, instinctively aware that death waited to greet them at their final destination. *Is that their fate? Is that my fate? Can those wheels be stopped?*

Stefan had said, "They must be stopped."

But how could you stop Hitler?

LILY

When our train pulled into the station in Sofia, I flashed back to that horrible scene in Skopje: Women screaming, kids crying. Police violently pushing and beating the few men who resisted. And that pale woman with an oddly empty stare, as if death had already taken her.

So many civilians, like me, had done nothing—just watched as if it weren't real.

Even worse—I worked in the office that planned it all! I helped make it happen!

By the time we'd made it back to the KEV office on Dundokov Street, Belev's callous words had somehow flipped, and now it was a voice in my head that repeated:

People will die regardless, but we can either be on the right side or the wrong side.

I wanted to be on the right side.

Ten minutes later, I was taking notes in a closed meeting with one German officer and three Bulgarian KEV operatives in Belev's office. Among the many logistical details about round-ups, holding centers, train schedules, and deportation timelines, one date was repeated and confirmed many times: March 10.

That was the day that 20,000 Jews within the traditional boundaries of Bulgaria would be hurriedly evicted from their homes, gathered at stations, and deported to Lom on trains. From there they would be put on boats and taken up the Danube River to camps in Poland.

Death camps—though they didn't use that word, I now knew that was what they were.

My chance to do something to help had arrived faster than I'd imagined.

Though fear shot through me at the idea of leaking this information—the distinct possibility of losing my job, being imprisoned, or worse—I thought of all of the lives I could save. And I heard my internal voice repeat:

We can either be on the right side or the wrong side.

From that moment, I didn't decide much consciously.

As negligent as it might sound, I didn't think through the options, make a strategy, or evaluate the pros and cons. It just came to me as I sat there at my desk at KEV headquarters.

I would *tell someone.*

A name and a face came to me. Dr. Levi. My doctor.

He was a kind, brilliant Jewish family man whom I would never wish any harm upon.

So it became very simple: Belev and the people I worked for planned to kill Dr. Levi, his family, and countless more innocent Jewish people. I couldn't sit there and do nothing about it.

I called Dr. Levi's receptionist to say I'd be dropping by for a checkup on the way home from work that evening around six o'clock. She sounded suspicious on the phone, probably because there had recently been a crackdown on Jewish-owned businesses. Most had already been shut down. Only a few were allowed to remain open. Dr. Levi's was one of the few.

When I entered the doctor's private office, I wasted no time.

"Doctor, I need to share information with you that is highly classified, but could save many lives."

He gazed at me, dumbfounded.

"Lily, what—"

"I need to know that I can trust you completely," I said, my voice shaking.

"I've taken an oath, darling," he said, pointing to a framed certificate in Latin on the wall behind him. "If this is about saving lives, your words are safe with me."

"On March 10 . . ." I began, and explained the rest. *Twenty thousand forced evictions. Round-ups. Trains. Mass deportation. Straight to death camps.*

Speechless for a few seconds, Dr. Levi stared at me in what must have been pure disbelief. Once convinced that I was not joking and that my place of work made me a credible source, he thanked me profusely. He hugged me and fought to hold back tears.

Before I'd even left the room, Dr. Levi was on the telephone, alerting others.

It felt good.

But now it was official:

I am a spy.

PETER

Late that night, from the kitchen, I listened to the adults speaking around the fireplace in our living room. The group included my father, Uncle Gancho, Mr. Ivan, Mr.

Cohen (David's dad), and Mrs. Vladka. All respected people from our neighborhood. Earlier that evening, the Jewish elders had received warning phone calls from Sofia and had called an emergency gathering at the synagogue to share the inside information: the forced deportation of Jews from a few Bulgarian cities was set to happen on March 10, and Kyustendil was on the list. It was supposed to have been a secret, but there had been a last-minute leak.

There were maybe only a thousand Jews in the entire city, and none held government seats or positions of power. *Why them?*

The group in my living room argued about what were facts and what was gossip, then about what they would do when armed soldiers actually showed up at their doorsteps. Soldiers had already been sighted on the streets that afternoon. Curfews were now being enforced, along with the new anti-Jewish property laws.

It had swept into our town like a wave, and everyone knew what was coming next.

Everything seemed futile, hopeless—and dangerous. Just the fact that Jewish people were in our non-Jewish house at that hour of night was in violation of the curfew law.

What would happen if we resisted?

Mr. Cohen and Mrs. Vladka looked at the others in the room for any answers that seemed more reasonable than suicide. They discussed possible solutions, from outright escape to legal appeals to the local government and police.

Then my uncle Gancho said, "This is much bigger than the local authorities! Orders must be coming from

Berlin straight to Sofia. We need to gather a delegation and travel to the capital to speak directly with Parliament member Dimitar Peshev—the representative for our district. He's a good man."

"What can Peshev do?" Mrs. Vladka asked.

"A delegation?" Mr. Cohen said.

"Yes, as many as we can gather," Uncle Gancho told Mr. Cohen.

"Jews and Gentiles united," my father added. "They can't ignore all of us."

"Young man, trust me," Mr. Cohen said to my thirty-six-year-old dad, "they *can* ignore us, and do much *worse* than ignore us!"

"Let's get the word out to meet on the corner of Tsar Simeon Street on Monday morning at seven o'clock," Gancho said. "We can all take the early train to Sofia."

"I'll make some calls," my dad said.

"Me too," added Ivan. "Hundreds will know by tomorrow."

"Wait, geniuses!" Mrs. Vladka said. "Did you forget about the curfew? Jews can't leave the city—especially not in one huge group. Are you kidding?"

"She's right," Mr. Cohen said.

My father stood up. "Then *we* will represent you. You're our neighbors. Our friends." His words and manner were very confident.

All eyes were on my dad. I slid from the kitchen doorway into the living room to get closer.

"To stand up for you is the least we can do," he finished.

Uncle Gancho nodded at Mrs. Vladka and David's dad. So did Ivan.

"Let's make phone calls all day Sunday," Ivan said. "We'll be two hundred strong by Monday morning!"

I stepped forward. "I'm coming with you guys!"

"No, Peter," my dad replied, not even looking at me. "You're too young, son. Go back to bed."

MARCH 8, 1943

MISHO

That same train packed with human beings rolls by in slow motion. I see the faces of my mother and sister through the cracks of those train cars. Their hands reach for me. I hear their voices.

In a cold sweat, I woke up to Archbishop Stefan banging on my door. Usually such a rude awakening would have bothered me, but my nightmare made me grateful for his interruption.

Stefan opened the door wide and the hallway light poured into my small, spartan seminary room.

"Misho," he said. "Please be ready to go by 7:30 AM. We have an important visit to make."

"Okay, Archbishop," I said groggily. "Where are we going?"

"We're going to see the king," he said.

I rubbed my eyes, still half asleep.

"King Boris?" I asked.

"Yes," Stefan replied. "I spent all day yesterday trying to contact him. Finally, I got through. He's at his mountain villa in Borovets, so have the car ready for a snowy trip."

I scratched my head. *Was I hearing him correctly?* The information wasn't fully registering. *It was freezing cold, still dark outside, and I was driving him where?*

"Did you say I'm driving you to see the king of Bulgaria?"

"Yes!" he bellowed and began to shut the door.

"Archbishop Stefan," I said, pausing his retreat. "Can I ask you one question?"

Stefan pressed his hand down on his crucifix. "Of course."

"Those people on the trains near Dupnitsa. What did they do wrong?"

Stefan winced and moved his hand to his beard.

"Nothing," he said. "They did absolutely nothing wrong, Misho."

"Were my—" I began and heard my voice crack. "Are my mother and sister safe?"

"Yes. They're safe in the convent. I checked last night."

"Thank you," I said and exhaled in relief.

"Now get ready. Today is an important day."

PETER

Monday morning I got up extra early. I put on my best clothes, threw on a small backpack, and jumped out of my second-floor bedroom window. That may sound dangerous, but I'd done it a hundred times to meet my friends or play football in the street. I hopped down to a dividing wall first and then to the ground, slipped through our backyard, and walked down a side street to avoid being seen. When I circled around to the corner of Tsar Simeon and Tsar Krum Street, I expected to see a huge crowd of people waiting. Hundreds. To my surprise and disappointment, I saw only two people: my dad and uncle Gancho. *The grand delegation!*

Confused, I hid behind a corner and waited for

others to gather there.

Five whole minutes passed, and then Mr. Ivan showed up.

Nobody else.

Where were the hundreds of good residents of Kyustendil?

I assumed my dad would be angry and send me straight back home, but I figured it was worth a shot. If I was going to help David, I had to try.

As I crossed the street in their direction, they turned their attention toward me.

"Peter, what in the hell are you doing here?" Dad said.

"I want to come."

"I already told you *no*."

Feeling daring, I peered up and down the empty street. "Where is everybody else?"

The three men looked at each other, as if none of them wanted to answer.

My dad made a growling noise.

"This is it," Gancho finally said. "Many of them are probably scared, and with good reason. We'll be going straight into the belly of the beast."

"There will be more Nazi patrols in and around Sofia," Ivan added.

"What does that mean?" I asked.

"It means things are getting very dangerous, Peter," my dad said. "Now go back home."

But my mind was set. I wanted to do something, anything, to help save David and his family. My neighbors. My best friend.

"Please," I begged. "You need more people. Four is

better than three, and a younger face might get some more sympathy."

"Are you calling us *old*, you little twerp?" my uncle Gancho jabbed.

Ivan laughed, a bit too loudly. It seemed like his nerves were getting to him.

My uncle leaned over and whispered into my dad's ear.

Resolute, I stood there on the curb—uncertain how I could help, but 100 percent ready for action.

My father read my eyes for a few crucial moments.

"Come on, son," he said finally. "Let's go."

He grabbed my shoulder and squeezed it hard. It was his sign of affection.

At 7:05 AM, the four of us walked down Tsar Simeon Street toward the Kyustendil train station.

MISHO

It snowed on the drive up the mountain to King Boris's villa. It was the first time I'd driven in snow, so I was nervous on the steep switchbacks.

Bishop Stefan didn't talk much on the way up. He mostly stared out the window and hummed an odd dissonant tune to himself.

After many cautious twists and turns, I pulled the car into the pine-tree-lined driveway. *Am I really driving up to the King of Bulgaria's house—as a chauffeur named Misho, no less?* I'd never admired royalty much, and I wondered about the extent of his power. I assumed the king's authority was mostly outweighed by the Bulgarian

Parliament and Hitler, but maybe it was more than that. Obviously, Stefan believed that he had enough influence to do something about the deportation of the Jews—unless it was already too late.

Of course, I didn't think I'd go inside and meet the king, which is why I remained relatively calm as I parked the car. No doubt I'd be asked to wait outside in the freezing car, which didn't sound pleasant, but didn't scare me either.

"Thank you, Misho," Stefan said, clearing his throat. "Now grab your coat. You're coming in with me."

"What?" I said.

"You heard me. I'm not having you freeze your ass off out here. Let's go."

By that point, I'd heard Stefan curse a few times. I didn't know if it was an old non-priestly habit, or something he'd taken to recently because of the stresses of war.

Either way, it didn't fit my image of an archbishop. I put on my coat and walked up the stairs toward the villa right next to the black-robed holy man.

We waited at the grand front door. My breath quickened and gave my nerves away.

"Relax," he said. "He won't come to the door himself."

The door was opened by an ancient, pencil-thin butler who escorted us through the entry hall to a large living room archway, where King Boris stood in a tweed suit.

"Welcome," he said.

"King Boris, thank you for inviting me."

"Did I have a choice, Archbishop?" the king said with a chuckle. "Who is your young friend?"

"This is my driver, Misho."

"Hello, Your Majesty," I said.

King Boris smiled at me. "No majesty here, just a sidelined king."

"Please, Boris, you're much more than that," Stefan said. "And now you have the chance to prove it to the world."

"I see you waste no time, Archbishop," the king said. "Come in."

"Frankly, Your Highness," Stefan said as he moved through the arched doorway. "There's no time to waste." He motioned for me to sit on a small, plush sofa just outside of the living room, and the two men walked into the luxurious parlor.

To my surprise, they didn't close the French doors, and they sat down no more than seven meters away from me. Though I could not see them from where I sat, I could hear them clearly.

"I know what you're going to say, Stefan."

"Of course you do, it's no secret now. But you didn't see the train I saw in Dupnitsa."

"I've heard. You're not the first to tell me."

"It's not only an abomination against God," Stefan said. "It's a disgrace to this nation."

"Yes, I agree, but there is a quid pro quo with Hitler."

"Listen to yourself, Boris. 'With Hitler,' you say. Is that who you want to be standing next to in the history books? He is just a man. He's not a god."

"He expects—" The king stopped. "The Germans expect full cooperation."

"An alliance, yes, which serves a practical purpose for them and for us," Stefan said. "But how does killing thousands of Jews serve anyone?"

"They're not being killed, Stefan. They're being sent to labor camps to work for the war effort."

"For the love of San Sebastian, Boris, are you blind?"

"Are you using a holy name in vain, Archbishop?"

"Yes! But I'm only invoking such a reference because this is the most important matter I—we—have ever faced!"

"You must be joking," the king said.

"No!" Archbishop Stefan nearly shouted it. "To stand idly by while your fellow men—fellow citizens—are murdered for nothing more than their religious beliefs? Their heritage? Their existence? Never!"

There was a weighty pause.

"How are you so certain they're being killed?" the king asked.

"After Dupnitsa, I called every priest between here and the Danube. I told them to be on the lookout for these trains filled with Jewish refugees. One priest from Lom called me back late that night and told me he had just witnessed them pull a dead man from the train car by his wrists. He watched soldiers beat other men with batons. One soldier shot a woman in the back simply because she wouldn't stop screaming for her daughter!"

"My God," the king said.

"They herded them all onto boats like animals and sent them up the Danube," Stefan added. "It's unfathomable, and it's happening in our own country."

"It's very unfortunate," said the king.

"Unfortunate?"

"I'm in a difficult situation, Stefan."

"Of course you are—you're the king!" the archbishop said. "Didn't Voltaire say, 'With great power comes great responsibility'?"

"Yes, but I can't fix everything."

"King Boris, with all due respect, God will not look kindly upon those who fail to protect their fellow man."

"Is that a threat, Archbishop?"

"No, no," Stefan said. "But God's judgment should concern you—should concern us all."

"Really? This from a holy man who just profaned Saint Sebastian a minute ago?"

"I'm confident," Stefan asserted. "That our all-powerful God is much more concerned with the life and death of thousands of human beings than one man's poor choice of words." He took a deep breath and added: "Actions, Boris. Actions."

Their conversation stilled for a minute. Then I heard the clanking of bottle to glass and the gurgle of liquid being poured. Liquor, I imagined. *Rakia*, probably, the archbishop's favorite. I wanted to crane my head around the corner and see their faces, but I didn't dare move.

The king finally spoke. "Well, Archbishop, I'm sure you're familiar with the line: 'All that matters is faith'? I'll take my cues from the Bible and have my peace with God."

After a long pause, Archbishop Stefan responded. "Boris, that line from the Book of Galatians is 'All that matters is faith expressed through love.' How will you show your love for your people—through inaction? By ignoring the issue? Praying in this protected villa up on a mountain?"

A heavy silence hung between them.

"You are a strange type of holy man," said the king.

"Your Majesty, I've learned this truth over the years:

holiness is nothing in isolation. It's easy to be reverent in a solitary room. In fact, that's when it's most convenient to us. The true test is how you apply your faith to others out in the world. Actually, the Letters of James said it best. 'So too, faith by itself, if it is not complemented by action, is dead.'"

King Boris sighed uneasily.

"You have the chance to save thousands of innocent lives, Your Majesty."

"Now you're calling me Majesty?"

"If that's what it takes," Stefan said.

The king laughed uncomfortably. "How can I save them?"

"You're the king, not me."

"Archbishop, surely you are aware of the current power-sharing arrangement with Parliament? Interior Minister Gabrovski and that fascist Filov are calling most of the shots now."

"Gabrovksi and Filov, huh? I guess I was wrong then." Stefan's tone was doubtful. "I was under the impression that you had the final word on national matters of great importance."

"Well, I do. I suppose. But it's more complicated now with the Germans involved."

"Is it? Even for the king?"

"I see what you're doing, Stefan."

"What?"

"Archbishop, is there such a sin as spiritual manipulation of the political sort?"

"Never," Stefan said.

The king chuckled.

"Perhaps this is an old tradition between royalty and

the church?" the archbishop offered.

"Perhaps," the king said skeptically, "but I don't like the feeling of it."

"Maybe what you feel, King Boris, is that uncomfortable voice in your heart telling you the difficult, yet *right* thing to do."

Frozen on the hallway sofa, I realized that my mouth was hanging wide open in amazement. I closed it but still couldn't believe the conversation I was overhearing.

Their last words came softly.

"I'll think about it," the king said. "And pray."

"May God guide you," Stefan said.

Moments later, Archbishop Stefan walked out and motioned to me. I jumped up and followed him out the door without saying goodbye to the king, who must have remained seated in his opulent living room.

Outside, the wind was severe and the air icy. Archbishop Stefan didn't say a word until we had sat down inside the frosty car and closed the doors.

"Did you hear any of that, Misho?"

"Well, some of it, but not very much."

"Don't lie to me."

I placed my hands on the frigid steering wheel. "Yes, I heard all of it, Archbishop," I said, expecting a reprimand or some kind of penance.

"And . . ." Stefan said, "do you think he'll do it?"

"Do what?"

"Save the Jews? Stop these damned trains?"

"I don't know," I said, "I couldn't tell."

Why would a monarch with waning authority make an effort to save less than one percent of his country's population? Was the king sufficiently religious that his conscience would actually absorb the archbishop's words? Would he dare stand up to Hitler? It was impossible to tell.

In the backseat, Stefan stroked his untamed beard and grumbled, "Me neither, kid."

LILY

The office was a frenzy of activity that day.

Tons of papers crossed my desk—orders, directives, addendums to be immediately sent by telegram to Dupnitza, Plovdiv, Kyustendil . . . every city marked for the first phase of deportations. One paper that caught my eye was simply a list of the names and addresses of prominent Jewish males' addresses in Sofia. The order was to arrest them in their homes as soon as possible. They were considered threats because of their ability to organize their community or contact people with power and influence. They were to be silenced and imprisoned. Maybe even killed.

"Lily!" Belev yelled through the open door of his private office, no more than three meters from my own desk.

"Yes?"

"Come in here, please."

Startled, I immediately went to his office, where two officials sat. I glanced at their swastika armbands and close-cropped hair.

"Lily, can you file these documents in my cabinet?"

"Yes, of course."

I grabbed the documents off his desk and kneeled by the open lower cabinet. As I sorted and filed the papers,

I listened.

"And the progress at the collection centers?" Belev asked.

"All is going smoothly," one man said.

"The warehouses are set for tomorrow night," the other officer added. "The house arrest orders have already been made, local police are in line, and there's no travel permitted."

"Good," Belev said. "Any resistance?"

"None to speak of. But there are rumors, sir, that some Jews are talking about it."

"About the deportation plans?" Belev asked.

"Yes."

"How in the hell would they know already?"

"We don't know, sir."

"Goddamn it. It was supposed to be top secret!"

"Maybe there was a leak, sir."

Belev slammed his fist on the desk so hard that the noise shook my core.

"Lily!" he yelled.

His shrill voice sent terrifying chills up my spine.

How does he know?

"Finish filing later," he said. "Please leave and close the door."

"Yes, sir," I said with a nervous crack in my voice and an internal sigh of relief. Legs wobbly and my head spinning with questions, I walked back to my desk.

Does he suspect the leak came from this office? Would he ask me directly, or pretend not to know and lure me into a trap? Did he have someone follow me when I went to Dr. Levi's office?

If I were caught, how would he punish me? Prison?

Execution?

I sat at my desk, trying to slow my breathing and the pace of my pounding heart.

Staring at the list of Jewish names on the document in the center of my desk, I wondered if these people were truly threats, and if the word "arrest" was a code word for execution. If these names were released, how many people could I potentially save? I couldn't know for sure—probably would never know. But twelve names stared back at me in typed black ink. Notepad in hand, I began copying down the names of KEV's prime targets, starting with Ioan Goodman, and the rest followed. By the twelfth, my hand was shaking uncontrollably and the name was nearly illegible.

I ate lunch alone that day, two blocks off Dundokov Street. Dr. Levi's office was only three blocks away. I went the long way, going six blocks out of my way to make sure nobody was following me. Heart racing, but with nobody in sight, I entered the doctor's office and his receptionist let me straight in.

I handed Dr. Levi the paper with the list of names. Then I asked him for a doctor's note in case I needed an excuse for being late back to work.

"Of course, Lily."

"Thank you," I said as he handed me the note.

"No, thank *you*," Dr. Levi said. "What you're doing is very brave—and extremely dangerous."

PETER

The military checkpoint at the Sofia train station loomed

in front of us. But the Bulgarian soldiers simply looked us over and waved us through. Seconds before, the conversation between Ivan, Uncle Gancho, and Dad had stopped, and the nervous silence continued as we four boarded the tram to the city center. When we pulled into downtown, I was hit by the sight of swastika flags ominously displayed on buildings and military vehicles. My heart plummeted into my stomach. Though none of us were Jewish or were technically breaking any laws, the fact that we were there to represent Jewish friends and defend their lives made me feel like a renegade—a freedom fighter.

With that title came risk. If the wrong authorities caught wind of our plan, we'd be arrested immediately.

And what was our plan? To meet the Cohens' friend, Ioan, downtown. He would help set up the meeting with Parliament member Dimitar Peshev. If Peshev agreed to meet with us, then my father, Ivan, and Gancho would inform him of the planned deportations on March 10, plead their case, and hope he could do something. Anything.

We reached Ioan's apartment building and front door without incident. He gave us all big hugs and offered us coffee. His place was warm and welcoming. A stout elderly man—Ioan's neighbor, Dimo—sat in the living room, ready to speak with us. We all sat down.

"It's good to see you, gentlemen, but where's the delegation?" Ioan asked.

We looked at each other in sympathy.

"*We* are the delegation," my dad said to Dimo and Ioan. "Just us. We expected more like a hundred, but they must have gotten scared by the enforced curfew and rumors."

"Rumors?" Ioan asked.

"Of the police arresting anyone obstructing the Laws for the Defense of the Nation."

Ioan nodded uneasily.

"And who's the boy?" Dimo asked.

"That's my son," Dad said.

"This is no work for a kid," said Dimo.

"I'm not a kid," I said.

I didn't want to offend my elders, but I also didn't want to be treated like a child. It was at that moment that I officially stepped into the arena of men. I could speak up for myself and deal with the consequences, but would entering manhood be as simple as declaring, "I'm not a kid"?

"Peter, please," my dad said. He turned to Dimo and Ioan. "Our neighbors are the Cohens—a Jewish family that you know well, Ioan. They couldn't come because of the new fascist laws. My son's best friend, David, might lose his home, his family, and his life. So he's here for his best friend. We are all here to represent the Jews of Kyustendil the best we can."

"Thanks for coming," Ioan said to us.

Dimo nodded with his arms crossed over his belly. "Not much of a delegation," he said.

"No, but hopefully—" Gancho began.

"—The power of our words changes their minds," I said. I was slowly, awkwardly, finding my voice.

"Power of words, huh?" said Dimo. "Who brought Mr. Naivete? And change *whose* minds, exactly?"

"The Parliament," my dad said. "That's why we came from Kyustendil. Our representative in Parliament,

Dimitar Peshev . . ."

"Yes, I've heard of Peshev—your holy savior!" said Dimo, throwing his hands in the air.

"Sarcasm won't help us here," Ioan told his crotchety neighbor.

"Do you know that our Parliament is led by pro-Hitler fascists—Gabrovski and Filov?" Dimo said, leaning in.

"He has a point," Ioan added. "This won't be easy."

"We have to try," my dad said firmly.

"Peshev is a good man," Gancho noted. "I met him once. We just need to get a meeting with him. Tonight or tomorrow."

"Tonight or tomorrow?" Dimo scoffed.

"Tonight or tomorrow," Gancho repeated, pronouncing it extra clearly.

"I understand what you said," Dimo said. "I'm not stupid. I'm simply pointing out that your master plan is beginning to look not only naive, but impossible."

Dimo's pessimism stifled the room.

Usually I didn't like speaking in front of groups of adults, but it just came out. "Anything is possible," I said.

Dimo sighed at the cliché, but Uncle Gancho smiled at me and my dad grabbed my shoulder and squeezed.

Ioan stood up from the couch and winked at me. "Let's not waste anymore time, then," he said. "I know someone who works in his office. I'll get his number and call Peshev. Tonight."

"What do we have to lose?" Ivan said, the first words out of him since we'd arrived.

"Your lives!" Dimo interjected. "They'll brand you all as traitors."

"Who's they?" Gancho said.

"The government, wise guy," he barked back. "You'll be talking directly to government officials. That is, if you even get a meeting."

With that, Dimo heaved himself up, walked out, and shut the door behind him.

Though I didn't like the cynical guy, he had compelled me to speak up in a room full of adults—something I hadn't done before. That day, I learned a lot about growing up.

LILY

It had sunk in.

I'm a spy.

Multiple nerve endings sent shivers through my neck and arms. I could no longer see myself in any other way—I'd leaked information not once, but twice. This time it was a specific list of names. Wouldn't Belev and his officers get suspicious when these particular Jewish citizens disappeared from public view or vacated their homes right before their arrests were ordered?

Sunset quickly turned to night. Over half of the desks on our floor were vacant, so I decided to leave work. The light was on in Belev's office; I assumed that, as usual, he'd be working late, obsessing over his plans for the upcoming mass deportation. Tens of thousands of people in multiple cities. From forced evictions to property confiscation—along with policing the masses on their way to train stations and then organizing travel from each transit center out of the country—it was a logistical nightmare. Belev was managing all of it.

I hit Dundukov Street full of nervous paranoia. Men in suits eyed me as they passed by, and some military guys stared. Any of them could have been assigned to watch me, to track my movements. Anybody or nobody. I dug my hands into my pockets and pulled my favorite scarlet winter coat close to my body. Angling my head down, I began marching toward Nevski Cathedral, to my studio apartment off Shishman Street. Just before I reached the corner, I bumped into a uniformed man on the sidewalk and nearly screamed.

It was Belev.

How in the hell had he gotten to the street so fast?

He grabbed my shoulders gently. "Why, Lily, you looked as if you've seen a ghost!" he said. "It's just me."

Did my haunted expression give me away?

"Sorry, you startled me."

"Why is that?" he asked gently. It was a sharp contrast from the pure rage I'd seen in him yesterday.

"I don't know," I replied tensely. "I'm never that comfortable walking alone at night."

"Well, can I walk with you, then? As your bodyguard?"

"Sure."

What else could I say? I couldn't say no.

My boss stared at me as we walked, but I kept my eyes steady on the ground, as if my only option was to concentrate on the pathway ahead. Really, I had found it difficult to look him in the eye ever since that train ride from Skopje. Since then, I'd kept my interactions with him to a minimum.

"Lily, are you okay?"

"Yes, fine. Thank you."

"Is there anything you need to tell me?"

"What?"

There's no way he knows already. Impossible.

"Something weighing on you?" Belev asked.

"Pardon me?"

Maybe he does know and he's just toying with me?

"Anything of concern coming from the office?" Belev said.

"Nothing in particular."

"Well," he said. "Morale seems low."

No, he doesn't know. He can't.

"Morale?" I said.

"Yes, or is it something else?" he asked.

He's just making conversation now, right?

"It has been stressful. Lots of work lately."

"Yes, that makes sense," he said with a nod. "What else is new, Lily?"

"Excuse me?"

He never talks to me so casually. Is he trying to flirt with me?

"Anything new going on in your life?" he said. "If you don't mind me asking."

"No, nothing much."

"No special someone? Boyfriend?"

"No," I said.

Damn it, I answered too quickly! This man should not know that I'm single.

"I see," he said with a smirk. "That's a very nice red coat. Classic."

My stomach churned, uneasy. Now it was obvious. He was flirting.

"Thank you," I said.

I knew nothing at all about Belev's life. Was he married or single? Did he have any kids? I guessed he was in his late thirties or early forties—way too old for me. But why was I even thinking these things? He repulsed me on so many levels. He was my boss, at least fifteen years older than me, and his job was to mastermind the extermination of all of Bulgaria's Jews! And I was now undermining all of his work and technically betraying him. For the first time, I considered my next move: if he was attracted to me, I could either reject him outright and risk the fallout, or I could be smart and act friendly to cover myself and stay in his good graces.

We neared the corner of Shishman.

"I can make it home fine from here, Mr. Belev."

"Sure thing," he said.

"Thanks for the escort."

"Good night, Lily."

I turned toward home and didn't look back, though I instinctively sensed his eyes watching me walk away. A mild nausea came over me. It wasn't merely the thought of Belev's romantic gestures that disgusted me. It was the idea building inside me—the idea of compromising myself, of yielding to his desires in order to save my own life.

No . . . never.

MISHO

The seminary courtyard in front of the archbishop's residence was so peaceful at night. It seemed thousands of miles away from war at that moment. But the simple act of looking toward the sky reminded me of the vast spaces of a world I couldn't explore. I was confined—stripped of freedom, religion, identity, family. I couldn't help but think of my mother and sister, Tatya, hiding in a dingy convent in the hills near Plovdiv. Were they getting on well, or suffering in solitude? Were they reciting the Amidah together, or forced to hide every single aspect of their Judaism?

I pulled a pack of cigarettes from my pocket I'd found hidden under the bed in my room. The seminary boarder before me had a secret habit and must have relocated in a hurry because he left a decent stash behind, complete with plenty of matches. I'd tried smoking a few times before with my high school friends, but never liked it.

I lit my first cigarette, took a drag, and gazed up at the tiny sliver of a moon. Then I coughed hard and fast. My throat burned like hell. But something about the pain drew me back to it. The next few inhalations were less harsh, my coughing less intense. I could focus on the smoke—inhale, exhale—and nothing else. The perfect distraction.

Until I heard footsteps crunching over gravel in the dark.

"The waxing crescent moon beckons you." Stefan emerged from the darkness. "Or is it the nicotine?"

"Probably both," I said and glanced at my cigarette. "Is this okay, Archbishop?"

"Of course," he said, taking a deep breath. "Can you spare one for me?"

"Sure." Surprised, I handed him a cigarette and lit it.

"You're a fan of the stars and the moon?"

"I guess you could say that," I said.

"Beautiful, yes," Stefan said, "but there's something unsettling about them, too."

"What's that?"

"The unknown. So much of the universe is unknown. The stars shine bright, but they are far, far away. The moon is much closer . . . but there are things about it we will never know."

"Are you okay with that?" I asked. "Not knowing?"

"I have to be," Stefan said. "God is unknown. My job, my entire purpose, is to be a conduit to an entity that is a divine mystery, an unknown. That's why we have faith."

"I don't know if I could do that," I said. "I don't like not knowing."

"About the outcome of the war? Your fate? Your mother and sister?"

"Yeah," I admitted. "Just now, I was thinking about them."

"They're okay, Misho," he assured me. "They're safe. I'm telling you that *I* couldn't find their remote convent even with a map and Marco Polo by my side."

"Thanks, Archbishop."

I looked away, smoking silently.

"Where's your father, Misho?"

"He died when I was young," I said. "I barely remember him."

"I'm sorry to hear that."

The holy man remained standing there, scratching his beard with one hand and smoking a cigarette with the other. I couldn't tell if he was trying to comfort me, or if he was lonely himself—looking for basic camaraderie, even if I was a young twerp. Maybe he needed the same exact thing as me: a moment outside in the fresh air to clear one's head before going to sleep.

"Did you always want to be an archbishop? Like when you were younger?"

"No." He laughed, gazing at the moon. "But I knew I wanted to be an actor."

"Like in the movies, or on a stage?" I asked.

"No, Misho. An actor in the sense that we tend to fall into one of two roles in life. Actors or spectators. We're either on the stage most of the time, or sitting in the audience."

It was an interesting analogy.

"I didn't want to sit there and listen to someone else's sermon," he went on. "I wanted to make my own."

"The same way you want to do something to help the Jews?" I asked.

"*Need* to, not want to," Stefan said. "It's a moral and spiritual question God has asked of me. And it's an easy one to answer."

"Well, I want to do something, too, to save my own people," I said.

"I understand, but you are already doing something."

"What?" I said, a bit frustrated. "I'm driving you. I'm hiding. You are making history right now, trying to save thousands of innocent people, and what am I doing?"

"You just need to survive this, Misho."

"I want to do more than just survive."

"You don't understand. Simply surviving this war will be a feat in itself."

I shook my head and took a drag. My lungs smoldered, but no cough.

"I want to help my people."

"That's a good inclination, Misho."

"What can I do, then?"

"Help me," he urged. "Assist me. Stand by my side in this fight for justice! It's the only thing worth fighting for now."

I was less than satisfied with his answer, but it didn't take long to consider the alternatives. Hiding in somebody's stuffy attic, or being in a prison camp in Poland, for starters. Facing down a firing squad with no chance of self-defense, or driving a holy man around town in his quest to help save my people. *Not bad.* I took another drag from my cigarette.

"Tomorrow I have another early morning meeting," he said.

"With who?" I asked.

"The Interior Minister of Parliament."

"At his government office?"

"No, at Pod Lipite Restaurant," Stefan said and cracked a smile. "It's a surprise visit."

"Surprise?"

"Yes, in the sense that he doesn't know he's meeting with me."

"Interesting."

It seemed that the archbishop had done some behind-the-scenes questioning to find out where this government official had breakfast every Monday morning. Clever, but there was no guarantee he'd be there.

"This may seem odd," Stefan said, "but can I ask you a question I've been mulling over?"

"I don't know if I can be of any help," I said, "but yeah, of course."

"Is it okay—" Stefan began and then hesitated. "Is it a sin to deliberately deceive one person if it's for the good of many people? There's Biblical references aligned to such questions, but I want to know your opinion."

"I'm sorry, I don't know if I understand the question."

"In other words, would it be wrong to lie to a single sinner if it resulted in the good of all—maybe millions?"

"I guess it depends," I said.

"On what?"

"If the sinner's in total darkness," I offered. "If they don't understand that what they are doing is deeply wrong."

"What if that sinner was planning to allow, to be complicit in, the extermination of thousands of innocent human beings? Would you lie to him to save those people?"

"Yes, if you put it like that."

"Then, in this circumstance, is it okay to lie?" Stefan asked.

"Is this a trick question?" I said.

"No."

"Then yes," I said.

The archbishop sighed in a way that was impossible to interpret. He flicked his cigarette butt into a small tin trash can and began to walk away.

"Do you mind if I ask you something?" I said.

"Go ahead."

"You say a lot of things I wouldn't expect an archbishop to say. Why?"

"I've heard that before," he said. "And it's because I have no desire to be a normal archbishop."

He turned and walked back toward his residence, away from the momentary calm of the courtyard and eternal peace of the stars above.

"Good night, Misho," he said as he faded into the night.

PETER

It was getting late. We all waited at Ioan's house, scattered between the narrow balcony and kitchen. His wife and daughter had made us dinner and provided us with blankets and pillows to sleep on their living room floor. Ioan, who had left to run errands and make phone calls from a different location, came through the front door just before midnight with renewed energy. He asked Ivan, Gancho, my dad, and I to have a seat in the living room.

"It took some maneuvering," he said, "but I just spoke directly to Peshev!"

"And?"

"You have a meeting with him tomorrow at 9:00AM."

We all lit up with excitement.

"Great!" Gancho said.

"All of us?" my dad asked.

"All of you, yes," Ioan said. "But I will not go. I can't. I don't know if you noticed because we've taken down the Hamsa and put other religious items away, but we're Jewish. Our family name is Goodman."

"But you're the one who spoke with Peshev," Gancho said. "You're our connection."

"Yes, but I told him to expect you four, not me," Ioan explained. "Because of the restrictions on Jewish citizenship, my voice will not be heard anyway. And I might even be in danger of arrest. I can't take such a risk right now. I have my family to protect." He glanced at the bedroom door, behind which his wife and daughter slept.

"Where are we meeting him?" my dad asked.

"At his home. I have the address."

"But, like Dimo said, what if they see us as traitors?" Ivan asked.

"Peshev won't arrest you," Ioan assured him, "but there's no guarantee that he won't tell the authorities."

"Jesus, they might arrest anyone!" Gancho said. "It's hard to know these days."

"You now see the reality of defending Jews," Ioan said. He paused. "Imagine if you were Jewish. Put yourself in our shoes and try to feel that level of constant anxiety."

I'd been sitting there listening to the adults speak, and I sensed that their purpose and will to do the right thing was weakening. They'd discussed it and planned the delegation, and we'd all spent four hours on a train and made this effort to get to Sofia, and we had vital information to share that wasn't in the papers or being talked about anywhere except for some Jewish communities. Is this what adults did in a crisis? Talked but never actually did anything? We couldn't let fear get in our way.

"We have to go!" I blurted out. "We have to tell Peshev exactly what's planned on the tenth!"

"It's not that simple, Peter," Dad said. "Plus, you're not going anyway. Too risky. You're too young."

"Wait, brother," Uncle Gancho said. "We should take Peter."

My dad stared at Gancho in disbelief.

"He's young, but he has courage," Gancho said. "He has passion. We need as much of that as we can get."

My dad looked over at me and knew that Gancho had a point. Our delegation was already miniscule. Anything—anyone—could help.

"The four of us, then," Dad said.

Their words filled me with vitality and belief.

The men spent the rest of the night talking intensely about what they would say to Peshev the following morning, who would speak, how they would organize their proposal. I fell asleep on the sofa amid their anxious chatter, under a cloud of cigarette smoke.

MARCH 9, 1943

MISHO

I parked in front of Pod Lipite Restaurant at 8:00 AM. Stefan adjusted his priestly robe and sash as he exited the vehicle. He had heard from multiple inside sources that Interior Minister Gabrovski ate breakfast here, like clockwork, every weekday morning between 8:15 and 8:45 AM.

"Better to be here early," Stefan said. "I don't want to miss him."

"Who?" I said as I sat behind the wheel.

"The sinner I told you about last night."

I must have furrowed my brow in confusion. Stefan patted his beard around his neckline.

"Well, come on."

"Inside?" I asked.

"You'd rather be an actor than a spectator, right?" Stefan asked.

"What?"

"Remember what we talked about last night?"

"Yeah," I said.

"Then come on! *Hai-de, momche.*"

The archbishop and I walked in and sat at a table near the center of the dining room. The only other customers were two elderly men in the corner bench seats. Stefan ordered mish-mash and coffee. I ordered *banitsa*. The aged dark wood interior and red folk-patterned tablecloths suggested that traditional Bulgarian cuisine was their specialty. The fact that Gabrovski liked this place hinted at his nationalism, or at least a certain amount of cultural pride.

At 8:15 on the dot, our food arrived and Gabrovski entered alone.

He sat down at a small table not far from us.

Stefan turned to him with a smile.

"Good morning, sir."

Gabrovksi, balding with a thick mustache, eyed Stefan with curiosity. If he ate there every morning, then Stefan's sanctified presence was truly out of the ordinary.

"Good morning, Father."

"I'm Archbishop Stefan. Nice to meet you."

"Peter Gabrovski," he introduced himself. "Archbishop, I've heard your name before."

"I've heard yours as well, Mr. Gabrovksi."

"Well then. I hope it was in a good light."

"Nothing horrible," Stefan said, as smooth as could be. "Do you mind if I join you?"

"Sure, but I wouldn't want your friend to be deprived of company," Gabrovski said as he motioned to me.

"Oh, Misho? He's my driver and seminary student. He needs to get used to solitude."

The archbishop stood up, abandoning his untouched meal, and took a seat across from the nation's most influential politician. I nibbled on my pastry alone, head down, listening intently.

"May I ask why you wish to mix church and state this morning, Archbishop?"

Stefan laughed politely.

"Funny you ask, Interior Minister," Stefan said. "I'm less concerned about church and state and much more concerned with right and wrong."

"What are you speaking of?"

"The forced deportations."

Gabrovski pulled a wooden toothpick out of a small ceramic cup. He put it in his mouth and appeared to grind it in his teeth. "Deportations of whom?" His aggrieved tone hinted that he knew exactly what Stefan meant, but didn't want to admit it.

"Jewish citizens of Bulgaria," Stefan said. "I think you are aware."

"Sounds like a nasty rumor."

"It's not. I saw them myself, packed on cattle cars three days ago near Dupnitsa. I've heard reports of abuse. Murder, even. Priests in Lom said they've been sent up the Danube already. Thousands of them."

"Perhaps from the territories of Macedonia and Thrace? Not Bulgaria proper."

"Does it make a difference?" Stefan asked.

"They must have been considered threats to the war effort—to the nation."

"Women and children?" Stefan asked. "Threats to the nation? I saw them. I heard them screaming for help."

"Please, Archbishop, you're going to ruin my breakfast."

Mr. Gabrovski scanned the room, looking for a waiter to distract him from the uncomfortable conversation.

"Well, it may be inconvenient for your appetite, but I thought you might want to know that this nation—your nation, your government—is sending thousands of its citizens to be slaughtered."

"Not technically citizens," Gabrovski said. "The Laws for the Defense of the Nation have stripped Jews of their citizenship."

"I stand corrected," Stefan said. "Our nation is sending thousands of innocent *human beings* to be slaughtered. And you approve of this, Mr. Gabrovski?"

"Slaughter? Come on."

"Have you not heard Hitler's own words?" Stefan asked. "They're not sending them to recreational camps."

"It's not my call," Gabrovski said.

"Whose is it, then?"

"If you must know, Prime Minister Filov's—and a special committee," the annoyed politician replied. "Besides, the wheels are already in motion."

"They can still be stopped," Stefan said.

Gabrovski laughed at this idea, then dismay overtook his expression. "Archbishop, I hope you have not undertaken your own illegal crusade here"—Gabrovski looked at me deliberately—"to save some Jews yourself? That would be a criminal act and a very bad move for the Church."

My nerves tightened. Fear struck me in the gut with his implied threat.

But Stefan's focus on the politician only intensified.

"Bad move for the Church?" he repeated. "I beg to differ. I believe that being involved in helping to save the lives of thousands of human beings would result in a 'good move' for any organization in the long view. It's you and your Parliament that should be worried about bad moves."

"I think this conversation is over, Archbishop."

Stefan leaned forward, as if getting ready to prop himself up and leave Gabrovski's table, then stopped. "Has King Boris contacted you about this matter yet?"

"No, I haven't spoken with the king recently," Gabrovski said, rolling his eyes.

"Surprising," Stefan said. "I spoke with him yesterday and he told me he'd be calling you."

"Really? About what?"

"About halting the eviction and eventual execution of fifty thousand Jews. He knows how much it will hurt our country, the shame and international embarrassment, not to mention the damage to his own conscience."

"Unfortunately, it's not the king's call," the politician said confidently. "It's up to Filov."

"And which German official does Filov report to?"

"Excuse me?"

"You heard me," Stefan asserted. "It's no secret that the Germans are pulling the strings."

"A high-ranking official named Dannecker, though it's no concern of yours."

"Mr. Gabrovski, do you know who the king reports to?" Stefan asked.

"I don't know, but I suppose you'll tell me it's God?"

The archbishop chuckled and cleared his throat awkwardly without speaking a word.

"Please, Archbishop, the suspense is killing me," Gabrovski added derisively.

"King Boris meets directly with Adolf Hitler," Stefan told him. "He's done so at least twice that I know of. Does Filov have that grotesque 'honor'?"

"I do not know. And who do you answer to, Archbishop? Maybe I should contact him?"

"Good luck reporting me," Stefan said with a grin. "I do answer to God."

"God. I should've guessed again."

The politician's amused grin held a mixture of arrogance and insecurity.

"It's too bad I can't have a conversation with Him," Stefan said. "I can only approximate what He would tell me based on a little book called the Holy Bible."

"I've heard of it," the politician said sarcastically.

"Do you read the Bible, Mr. Gabrovski?"

"Not regularly, no." Gabrovski shifted in his seat.

"Well, there's a passage from the Book of Ephesians, Chapter Six, that's fitting. 'For we do not wrestle against flesh and blood, but against the rulers, against the authorities, against the cosmic powers over this present darkness, against the spiritual forces of evil in heavenly places.'"

Stefan stood up and pushed in his chair. "Mr. Gabrovski, I invite you to go up to a rooftop and gaze out on our city and this heavenly place that is our country. I implore you: Don't be the darkness that stains this great nation. Don't be the person who stood still and did nothing while evils were done to innocent people. You can do something monumental today."

Gabrovski repositioned the toothpick he was chewing, but didn't say a word.

"I know about the deportation orders for tomorrow, the tenth," Stefan added.

"What?" Gabrovski gasped. "How?"

"What's important is that the Church knows, and today more Bulgarians will learn of it and become upset. The king knows this, and he doesn't like the idea of a population in revolt."

"A revolt over Jews, huh?" Gabrovski replied.

"Is there any history of anti-Semitism in this nation?" asked the archbishop.

Gabrovski knew the answer was no, but he remained

silent. I'd lived my whole life in Bulgaria and had never felt the sting of discrimination until the government allied with the Nazis.

Just then, the politician's breakfast arrived. I noticed that he had never actually ordered; he was such a regular that they must have known his usual order and brought it without even asking. Clockwork. *Would such a creature of habit change his mind? Listen to an old clergyman?*

Gabrovski took the toothpick out of his mouth and placed his napkin on his lap.

"Bon appetit, Mr. Gabrovski," Stefan said.

"Good day, Archbishop," he replied almost mockingly, and adjusted his tie at the collar.

"Say hello to the king for me," Stefan added. "He should be contacting you shortly."

Gabrovski tsked his tongue.

Archbishop Stefan left four leva on our table and exited the restaurant. I followed him out, in shock at the archbishop's style of backroom diplomacy and the veiled threat that Gabrovski had floated my way. After ushering Stefan into the backseat, I sighed in relief as I plopped down in the driver's seat.

"Impressive," I said. "Was that the single sinner you mentioned last night?"

"We'll see," Stefan said. "He may redeem himself yet." Then he began to mumble, holding the crucifix that hung from his neck.

Would Stefan's words be enough to sway Gabrovski? Did he even have enough time?

It was ticking by. We had less than twenty-four hours.

PETER

Dimitar Peshev's apartment was surprisingly close to Ioan's neighborhood.

Walking next to my dad, Uncle Gancho, and Ivan, I was proud. These were the only men from my town who had the courage and strength of will to try and help others. I didn't realize it at the time, but they were totally unselfish in the risk they were taking. Maybe that's why nobody joined us, because most people were afraid and selfish.

In that moment, on that cold morning walk to Peshev's, I didn't question my choice.

The fact was, I didn't want to lose my best friend, David. Simple as that.

I wouldn't be able to live with *not* acting on his and his family's behalf—standing on the sidelines while soldiers took them away forever. No, fear didn't cross my mind that morning. As each steaming breath hit the freezing air, I became more alive than ever.

Mr. Peshev had a round face, a dark mustache, and an air of dignity. In an almost familial way, he greeted us politely at the door and led us into his living room, which was decorated simply and modestly. This wasn't the penthouse of a fat cat politician. I already understood why Uncle Gancho had called him a "good man."

Mr. Peshev gestured for us all to sit down. "I understand that you are here on behalf of your Jewish friends in Kyustendil," he said.

"Yes, we—" my dad began.

"That's admirable," Mr. Peshev interrupted.

"Well, we—"

Peshev cut him off again. "I'm aware of the problem with the Laws for the Defense of the Nation. I opposed it in Parliament. But I imagine you are witnessing the discrimination now firsthand, and are wondering why it is happening. Have they begun enforcing the property laws, too?"

"Yes, but we're most concerned about—"

"If the concern is about my representation of the people of Kyustendil," said Mr. Peshev, "I assure you that the Prime Minister Filov, Gabrovski, and others are responsible for this, not me. If your friends are losing their jobs or their property, I assure you that—"

"They're going to kill them!" I blurted out.

The room fell silent, and all eyes focused on me.

"Excuse me?" Mr. Peshev said.

"Please, Peter," my uncle whispered. "We can handle this."

"What's the boy talking about?" Mr. Peshev asked, with what appeared to be a shift from pre-packaged statements to a sincere curiosity.

My dad and Gancho explained, telling Mr. Peshev about what had happened in Skopje days prior—thousands of Jews forced from their homes and packed into cattle cars at the train station, resisters beaten by the police, families torn apart, and all of them shipped to Poland.

Peshev listened wide-eyed, leaning forward with his hands gripping his knees.

"Did you know about this, Mr. Peshev?" my dad asked.

"No," he said, clearly affected. "God, no."

My dad explained that the authorities were preparing

to do the same in Kyustendil and other cities. That all Jewish families were now under strict curfew, stripped of citizenship, and forced to wear the yellow Star of David patch or be arrested. That soldiers had cleared out an old tobacco warehouse right next to the train tracks. That forced evictions and deportations were scheduled for tomorrow.

"This is insane," Mr. Peshev said. "How do you know all this?"

"We've witnessed it," Gancho said.

"And what about March 10? How do you know the exact date?"

"They were trying to keep it secret," my dad said. "But there was a leak."

"Someone leaked the plans to a Jewish man in Sofia, and word spread," added Gancho.

"So there's a spy in the KEV?" Peshev said.

"What's KEV?" I asked.

"Ah, finally something I know that you don't!" Mr. Peshev said. "Funny how that works. The KEV must have kept this from Parliament to avoid any opposition. Those sneaky bastards."

I was puzzled. And by the looks of Ivan, Gancho, and my dad, I wasn't alone.

Peshev explained, "KEV is the department in charge of the so-called 'Jewish Question.' They were tasked with drafting the Laws for the Defense of the Nation, and overseeing enforcement. But up to this point they've kept a low profile. They never spoke publicly about new measures or deporting Bulgaria's Jewish population . . . but it sounds like it's already started."

"In Macedonia, yes," Gancho said. "Kyustendil,

Plovdiv, and Dupnitsa are next."

"That's why we're here," I said.

Peshev focused on me as if my voice was now equal to those of the adults in the room.

"We need to stop this from happening," I continued. "We all know what Nazis do to Jewish people. They send them away and . . ."

The men were silent.

Ivan finally spoke. "This would be the worst stain on Bulgaria in all its history."

"We were oppressed by the Turks for five hundred years," Gancho said. "We can't let our government become the oppressors of Jews."

Again, quiet filled the room, but I sensed an indignation building in Mr. Peshev.

"You're the only politician we know," I said without hesitation. "Can you speak to Parliament? Can you stop the deportations?"

"I don't know if I can," Mr. Peshev said, "but I'll be damned if I'm not going to try." He stood up abruptly. "And I know exactly who to talk to first."

LILY

At that hour in the morning, there were only a few employees in the KEV office. I'd only been at my desk for a few minutes when the phone rang.

I picked up the receiver. "Hello?"

"Is this the Komisariat for Jewish Questions office?" It was an unfamiliar voice, quite agitated, on the other end of the line.

"Yes," I said.

"Who am I speaking to?" he asked.

"Alexander Belev's secretary."

"Is he in the office?"

"Yes, he is, but may I ask—"

Click.

He cut me off by hanging up the phone.

Rude man. Is he looking for Belev, or for me?

I became anxious at the thought of this anonymous caller hunting me down because he knew something about me. *Am I on some kind of suspect list? Is this caller a policeman, or a government agent?*

Five minutes later, a lampshade-mustached man in a smart suit burst through the main door to our office. He was out of breath, as if he'd sprinted to our building.

His eyes locked on mine. "Are you the secretary?" he asked impolitely.

"Yes," I said, suddenly afraid.

"Where's Belev?"

"I'm right here," Belev said, standing in front of his private office as if he'd been cued to emerge. "Who might you be, and what's the matter?"

"I'm Dimitar Peshev, Parliament member from Kyustendil district," he said. "And I've heard some very disturbing news this morning."

"And how does this concern me?" Belev asked, narrowing his eyes.

"They're preparing to deport all the Jews in my city and elsewhere," Peshev said. "And you're in charge of this department! Did you plan this?"

"Why, yes, of course we did," Belev replied arrogantly.

"Without approval of Parliament?"

At that moment, I recognized that this man, Peshev, wasn't angry. He was passionate about an act of injustice. *Our* act of injustice.

"Sorry you didn't realize, but we don't *need* Parliament's approval," Belev replied.

"Then on whose authority?"

"A gentleman by the name of Adolf Hitler."

Peshev placed his hand on his forehead, seemingly in frustration, but proceeded with an unexpected equanimity.

"Well, then, Mr. Belev, when do you plan on telling the Bulgarian people that we are all subjects of Hitler's Third Reich? Because we're all under the impression that our government aligned with the Axis in order to maintain our own sovereignty and expand our national borders—not to take orders from Nazis and send tens of thousands of our own citizens to their deaths."

"You exaggerate, sir," Belev said.

"Exaggerate what?"

"Labor camps are hardly death sentences, and this is a matter of national security."

Belev shot me a harsh glance—clearly saying *shut up*, just in case I considered exposing the grim truth. Peshev noticed. I wanted to shrink away and disappear.

"You know that's a lie, Mr. Belev," he said.

At this remark, Belev shrugged his shoulders dismissively. "That's your opinion."

"And my friends in Parliament will have a very strong opinion, too," Peshev replied.

"You can try, but I have to break the news to you," my boss said. "You can't stop the deportations. The wheels are already in motion, Mr.—what was your name again?"

"Peshev," he said. "Dimitar Peshev."

The fiery man spun around and left the building in a hurry.

Belev went into his private office, slamming the door behind him.

Less than a minute later, my phone rang again.

"Good morning, may I speak with Mr. Belev? This is Peter Gabrovski."

"Interior Minister Gabrovski?" I asked.

"That's correct."

I strode over to Belev's door and knocked. Though he was noticeably disturbed after the run-in with Peshev, he would not want to miss this phone call.

I opened his door. "Peter Gabrovski is on line two."

Belev hit the button on his phone and picked up. I lingered just inside the doorway.

"Yeah," Belev answered. He tapped a pencil on his desk as he listened a moment. "Yes, I just had the pleasure of meeting this Peshev!" he said sarcastically. "How the hell does he know about the deportations?"

Belev made many "uh-huh" sounds as Gabrovski spoke on the other end of the line. "Sure, witnesses could have seen some trains last week, but not the orders for March 10."

Suddenly he jumped to his feet. "Goddamn it! Who else knows?" After a brief silence he shouted, "Does classified information mean anything around here? Jesus!"

Belev slammed the phone down, red in the face as if he were about to erupt. He glared at me and pointed to the chair in front of his desk. Wary and jittery, I sat down.

"Lily, I'm going to need your help with something."

"Yes, of course, Mr. Belev," I said.

He hesitated and examined my face, as if wondering whether he should tell me.

"We have a *traitor* in this office," he said finally. "And we need to find out who it is immediately."

MISHO

That afternoon was intense. And it wasn't just because I spent the rest of the morning worrying about Mr. Gabrovski sending policemen to the seminary to come arrest me.

After lunch, in a rush, Archbishop Stefan asked me to drive him to a synagogue to pick up Rabbi Daniel Zion. The only thing he said on the drive over was that the rabbi was in grave danger and we needed to help him immediately.

We.

Was he including me just to make me feel like I was actually helping my own people now, or did he really mean it?

When we pulled up in back of the downtown synagogue, one that my mother had taken me to as a child, I spotted the bearded rabbi carrying a suitcase, already shuffling hurriedly toward our car.

"Leave the engine on, Misho. Don't get out!"

With an urgency I'd never seen in him, Stefan opened the back door and the rabbi threw himself inside, suitcase and all.

"Drive, Misho. Let's move!"

The rabbi was out of breath.

Was he being chased out? I stepped on the gas.

As I pulled the car around the corner, five or six

policemen at the entrance to the synagogue looked up and down the street. One spotted us, yelled, and pulled out his gun.

"Duck!" I yelled at the two clergymen in the backseat.

I lowered my head and stomped on the accelerator, keeping one eye on the road ahead. I heard the pop of a gunshot and then another. One of them hit our car. I imagined the next shot hitting me in the back of the head and my blood spurting onto the dashboard, but there was no next shot. After a few blocks, I made a screeching left-hand turn onto an empty side street, decreased our speed slightly, and took a deep breath.

"That was close," Stefan said as we raced away from the scene.

"They were inside the synagogue." Rabbi Zion said, panting. "Destroying things. Horrible desecration. For the love of God!"

"It's appalling, Rabbi," Stefan said. "But I'm so glad you called me. For now you can stay with us at the seminary. The police won't dare raid our property."

How could he be so sure? Did they get our license number? Wasn't this car registered? Harboring Jews was illegal. If they could run a peaceful, respected rabbi out of his own synagogue, then anything was possible.

"God bless you, Stefan," the rabbi said, then patted me on the shoulder. "And thank you for driving well, young man."

"This is Misho," Stefan told the rabbi.

"*Shalom*, Misho."

"*Shalom*, Rabbi Zion," I said.

My pronunciation must have given me away. "Him, too?" the rabbi asked Archbishop Stefan.

"Yes, the Church is trying to directly protect as many of our Jewish friends as we can, Rabbi," Stefan said.

"Bless your hearts."

As we neared the seminary, Stefan and Rabbi Zion reviewed the recent injustices.

"It must be difficult," Stefan said.

"Stripped of all respect," the rabbi said. "All so suddenly—just last week I was told not to worry."

I thought of how the archbishop had assured me not to worry about my mom and Tatya. That they were safe in a convent near Plovdiv. *Were they still safe?*

"I tried my best to influence the king," Stefan said.

"And?"

"I don't know," he said, his fingers combing his enormous beard. "Theoretically, he could make one phone call and change everything."

"But then he has Hitler to answer to."

"Unfortunately true," Stefan said. "I tried calling the king three times today, and nobody answered."

The rabbi shook his head.

"I spoke to Interior Minister Gabrovski early this morning," Stefan added. "He also could help prevent this travesty, that is if he—"

"Help prevent?" Rabbi Zion interjected. "The deportations have begun."

"Yes, I know of the Macedonian and Thracian tragedies," Stefan said somberly. "Misho and I saw one of the trains a few days ago."

"No, Archbishop—I mean here, today!" the rabbi said, surprised that Stefan didn't know. "I spoke with colleagues in Plovdiv an hour ago. They began rounding up people from their homes, schools, everywhere—they've been moved to transit centers and are only waiting for trains."

Stefan gasped. "It can't be happening already."

"It is!" the rabbi exclaimed.

Hadn't Gabrovski laughed when Stefan said we could stop the deportations? That bastard. He knew they were already happening.

Maybe the process had been expedited once they knew the word was out? Had Stefan's message to Gabrovski this morning had the opposite effect than he'd intended? Instead of feeling compelled to stop the deportations, could Gabrovski have accelerated them?

Within the walls of the seminary, I parked the car in front of the archbishop's residence.

"Misho, can you show Rabbi Zion to the free room at the end of the hall?"

"Yes, of course," I said, and got out to help the esteemed rabbi with his suitcase.

"I need to call Archbishop Kiril in Plovdiv immediately." Stefan turned and headed for his office faster than I'd seen him walk in the month I'd worked for him. Trepidation shot straight to my heart.

Deportations in Plovdiv.

PETER

After speaking to Mr. Peshev that morning, we spent the first half of March 9 waiting.

We had spoken the truth, and now there was nothing else to do but wait. Powerless.

My dad paced around Ioan's apartment impatiently.

Ivan and Uncle Gancho alternated between drinking coffee in the kitchen and smoking on the small balcony.

I needed a distraction to keep from worrying about David and his family. I picked up a book on Ioan's coffee table. *The Communist Manifesto.* I flipped through it, trying to make sense of the proletariat and the bourgeoisie class struggle. I didn't care about Marx's ideas—or at least the ones I could understand—except for one word that kept repeating: *revolutionary.*

Was this the only force that could stop injustice from continuing?

Was our only option to rely on politicians to help us? Was that the only way to protect my best friend from becoming a victim of the Nazis? Or was it time to take up arms and take to the streets?

Revolutionary. I liked the sound of it.

Ioan's phone rang, and we all assumed it was Peshev with some kind of news. Ioan called my father over to take the phone. He put the receiver to his ear, but didn't say much. All of us were glued to his facial expression. *Who was he talking to? Was it good news?*

No. Any glimmer of hope in his face disappeared almost instantly. Something bad had happened. Just like that, the call was over and Dad hung up the phone. I braced myself.

"Well?" Gancho said.

My dad looked at me. "That was your mother," he said. "Soldiers came for the Cohen family an hour ago."

"No!" I cried. "That's impossible!"

"All Kyustendil's Jews are being removed from their homes and taken to the warehouses by the train tracks."

"Jesus, one day early!" Gancho said.

My dad clutched his head. "I thought we had more time to stop this."

I jumped to my feet. "We should be back in Kyustendil. We can protest. We can fight back if we have to."

"Son, going up against the German and Bulgarian army is not the answer."

I looked to Gancho and Ioan for answers, anything, but they had none.

Powerless.

I hated the sound of it.

Ivan, Gancho, Ioan, and my dad quickly excused themselves and left the apartment. They said they were going out to smoke, but clearly they were going to discuss something they didn't want me to hear. I sat on Ioan's living room couch and fought the images rushing to my head: my best friend being pushed to the ground by a faceless soldier; his mother struggling in vain; his father pleading, trying to reason with the soulless monsters in dark fascist uniforms who were ripping them from their homes.

My eyes welled up. I wanted to scream, but not in this apartment in the middle of Sofia.

The phone rang.

It wasn't my house or my place to answer, but maybe it was my mom calling back.

I picked up and heard a familiar voice.

"Hello, this is Dimitar Peshev," he said. "To whom am I speaking?"

"This is Peter."

"The young man from this morning?"

"Yes," I said.

"Is your father or uncle around?"

"No, not at the moment, sir."

"Okay, well, I trust that you can relay a message to them."

"Of course, Mr. Peshev."

"I've spoken to a number of my colleagues in Parliament today, and many of them share my disgust at the news of the secret mass Jewish deportations," he said. "Many have agreed to sign a petition against the action as unconstitutional."

"That's great!" I said.

"Well, it's a start, but it may not help," Peshev clarified. "Tell your father and the others that I am meeting with Interior Minister Gabrovksi in the next few minutes to discuss the petition and make an appeal. He should have the power to stop this. Unfortunately, he and Prime Minister Filov are both pro-Nazi. But if they realize the secret is out and that the political backlash will be damaging to the war effort and their positions, they might be willing to stop it."

An unexpected rush of hope turned me tongue-tied. "Th-thank you, Mr. Peshev."

"I'm trying my best, Peter."

"This might sound stupid, sir, but is there anything I can do?" I asked, picturing my dad and the other adults outside smoking their cigarettes. "I can't stand just sitting here while this is all happening."

"For now, pray, Peter," he said. "Pray that Gabrovski will listen to me and that more concerned Bulgarians with influence will show their outrage at the thought of Nazis taking *any* citizen from our borders."

He hung up the phone.

Pray? That's not what Karl Marx would do.

LILY

Just after 3:00 PM, Mr. Belev requested that I accompany him to the office of Interior Minister Gabrovski. From the KEV office, it was about a five-minute walk to the Parliament building. Belev said he wanted me there to take notes, which I found odd. He'd never asked me to take notes in his meetings before. It made me suspicious that he was trying to keep me close to him so he could monitor me, or test my loyalty. The question haunted me every hour of the day: *Did Belev know I was the leak?* If so, he maintained quite a poker face.

We were sent directly into Gabrovski's office and the two men shook hands hastily. Gabrovski eyed my skirt and stockinged legs before acknowledging my face, then ignored me altogether. I sat on a straight chair in the corner and took notes.

"How is this happening?" Belev asked him.

"I was going to ask you the exact same thing."

"The plan was supposed to be kept top secret!"

I kept my head down and tried not to squirm in my seat. If my thoughts and feelings were shown, I'd be caught and crucified in a heartbeat.

Mr. Gabrovski ran his hand over his bald head.

"This was the exact thing we were trying to avoid," he said. "Now we have the Church and these goddamn Jewish rats spreading the word everywhere!"

"What's the difference, it's already started," Belev said. "The transit centers will be filled with the vermin by nightfall and the first trains will leave precisely at midnight. That was always the plan. Transport them in the darkness so nobody will see. No one will raise a fuss."

"Too bad that wasn't the plan last week when the archbishop saw trainloads of Jews being shipped across the country in broad daylight," Gabrovski said.

"Archbishop?" Belev snorted. "Who cares about an old priest?"

"Who cares?" Gabrovski raised his voice. "The Church spreads gossip faster than the radio!"

"You're scared of a few churchgoers raising hell?"

"You obviously don't hold an elected office, do you, Belev?"

My boss readjusted himself in his chair and crossed his legs arrogantly. "So, we'll speed it up," he said. "The trains will be loaded and gone before midnight. I'll give the rush order, and who cares what anyone says tomorrow? It will be too late."

Gabrovski paused and let out an extended sigh. "It's not that simple."

"Why's that?" Belev asked with growing exasperation.

"Parliament member Dimitar Peshev paid me a visit about an hour ago."

"That same bastard stormed into my office earlier today," Belev ranted. "Screw him!"

"Yes, well, he's already alerted almost forty other Parliament members who are signing a petition calling for an immediate end to the deportations."

"Prime Minister Filov will never allow it," replied Belev.

"You seem to be forgetting that Bulgaria is still a partial democracy."

"Yes, partial to us. Ha!" Belev laughed, thinking himself quite clever. "I'll speak to Filov. He'll have the final word."

It was hard to keep up. My pencil raced across the page, logging only the key words and phrases in the conversation.

"There's something else," Gabrovski added.

"Come on."

"There's something—someone—else we've overlooked."

"Who's that?"

"King Boris," Gabrovski said. "We haven't heard from him lately, but there are rumors that he's heard about the deportation of Jews and he's not too happy about it."

"Who told you that? Peshev?"

"No, Archbishop Stefan."

Belev paused. "It sounds like there are *two* people we need to get rid of."

The room went silent—so quiet that the sound of my pencil writing on my notepad suddenly became very audible.

Both men turned their heads toward me.

"Don't write that last part, Lily," Belev commanded.

Two people we need to get rid of.

"Of course not," I replied, my own heartbeat thundering in my ears.

MISHO

I was called to Stefan's dining room by one of the priests. Odd, because I usually had dinner with the monkish seminary students, never with the archbishop. Rabbi Zion met me at the door and led me to the plain, dark wooden dining table. Old candles crowded the centerpiece, a strong smell of wax emanating from them. Stefan, already seated, played with his beard that nearly reached the table's edge.

"Good evening, Misho." His tone was especially somber. "There is no easy way to say this . . ."

His words almost choked me, as if my whole heart was being pushed up into my tight throat. I looked over at the rabbi for some kind of hint, but he only gazed downward, obviously disconcerted.

"I spoke to Archbishop Kiril this afternoon," Stefan continued. "He told me the worst news possible, so brace yourself."

I can't.

"All of the Jews in Plovdiv were rounded up from their homes this morning."

No.

"I thought . . ." I started, not wanting to believe him. "I thought it wasn't supposed to happen until tomorrow."

"I know," he said. "But Archbishop Kiril said they started at the Jewish school and moved all the parents there, too. The roundup included Plovdiv and the surrounding areas."

I stopped listening. I didn't want to hear. My ears registered only a high-pitched ringing. My eyes focused only on one tarnished silver candle holder in the middle of the table.

Did Stefan's meeting with Gabrovski rush the deportation orders? By attempting to stop the situation, had he made things worse? And by hiding, by doing nothing, was I part of the problem?

"Misho, are you listening to me?"

"Yes," I said, turning my attention back to Stefan.

"They raided many church properties, including the convent," he said. "Your mother and sister were taken."

Breathe.

Breathe again.

Keep breathing.

Somehow I already knew Stefan would say those exact words. *Your mother and sister were taken.*

I couldn't make eye contact with him and simply stared down at my hands in my lap as if they were no longer attached to my body.

"Kiril will do everything in his power to stop them," Stefan continued. "He told me he would lay his body on the train tracks before letting the Jews be shipped away."

Would that really stop Hitler and the Nazis? What could any of us do? It was hopeless.

"We must have faith," the rabbi added.

I shook my head. *Faith? That's it? That's all you've got?*

Numb, I couldn't bring myself to say another word out loud. I needed to be alone. Immediately. I stood up and rushed out of the room.

Out in the courtyard, I tried to light a cigarette, but my trembling hands dropped it on the gravel.

That's when I started crying.

I should be with my mom and Tatya.

I should be holding their hands.

I should be there, too.

LILY

At around 6:00 PM, back at the KEV office, Alexander

Belev stormed out of his private office and barreled toward my desk.

"Let's go."

The command startled me. I was constantly on the defensive—terrified that all of the leaks were actively being traced back to me.

"Where?" I asked, trying to remain calm.

"To talk to this bastard—Peshev."

"Why me?"

"You'll see," he said.

Why does he want me with him? Does he know about Dr. Levi?

"Do you want me to take notes again?"

"No," Belev said. "I need you to be there so I don't do anything stupid, like try to kill this son of a bitch myself."

I had never seen Belev so intense and angry. Rage filled his eyes. He grabbed my coat from the rack and practically threw it at me. "Come on, Lily."

We both walked briskly across Dundukov, past Nevski Cathedral, and toward the Parliament building for the second time that day. Belev walked so fast that I struggled to keep up. Once inside the building, I followed him down a long hallway. He pounded on Peshev's office door three times, and then let himself in.

"Excuse me, your manners?" said Peshev, as he stood up from behind his desk.

"Shut the hell up about manners!" Belev barked.

I stood next to him, filled with anxiety. *Is he angry enough to actually do something violent?*

"What are you doing here?" Peshev asked, obviously surprised at the intrusion.

"Are you kidding me?" Belev said. "Now you're going to act like you haven't been making an effort to halt my entire operation."

"Your operation—you mean to kill all the Jews?"

Belev scoffed. "So crude, Peshev." He shook his head in disgust. "Do you really not understand? These people are threatening the country! They seek to undermine the war effort and our alliance with Germany—you seem to want our entire nation to implode."

"Give me one piece of evidence that Jews are threatening this nation," Peshev said.

"Spoken like a true traitor."

"Still waiting for evidence."

"You'll see the evidence when it's too late," Belev said, "if you continue trying to block our operation."

"So your evidence of a Jewish threat is based on nothing but fear . . . of the unknown future?"

"It's hardly unknown, *Peshev*." Belev spat his name out like a curse. "Hitler has conquered the entire continent because these European nations are weak. We're on the right side. We'll be strong again. You'll see."

"You're stupider than I thought, Belev."

"I beg your pardon?" Belev said, reaching for his belt. I was afraid he had a hidden handgun, but he only adjusted his waistline as if it helped him deflect the affront.

"Have you heard of Stalingrad?" Peshev asked rhetorically. "The Germans lost and are now in retreat on the Eastern front. Have you not read the papers? Or do you not know how to read?"

"I wouldn't throw insults so flippantly."

Peshev didn't say a word, but tilted his head slightly to one side and raised his brow as if to say, "Or what?"

"I also suggest," Belev continued, "that you stop trying to save the Jews from deportation. Gathering Parliament member support to reject a government mandate is against the law."

"And you don't think that killing tens of thousands of people goes against a higher law?"

"Stop with your virtues," Belev said. "It just shows your ignorance."

"My job is to represent the community of Kyustendil. And they do not want to send off their Jewish neighbors to be slaughtered."

"It's already happening. Tonight at midnight."

"There's still time, then."

Belev scoffed and chuckled. "Your path will become *very* dangerous."

"Are you threatening me?"

"You can take it as a strong recommendation to stop any actions that might prevent my office from doing its job."

"Your *job*?" Peshev repeated mockingly. "You act as though laying bricks and killing innocents are equivalent. And I'm sorry to say, but the only ignorant one here is you, Mr. Belev—and perhaps your little secretary there."

Peshev nodded to me and, for the first time, I didn't like him. Of course, he had no idea I was really on his side—and had likely tipped off the very Jews who had spoken to others in his native Kyustendil, who had then contacted *him*.

"You leave her out of this," Belev demanded.

As the irony of the situation deepened—my boss defending me without knowing I was the one who'd leaked information that threatened to halt his entire plan—my discomfort faded and the thought of saving thousands of innocent people warmed me.

But would they be saved? Peshev had tried, word was out—but would it stop anything? Would Jews still be put on trains at midnight?

"If you're finished threatening me, Mr. Belev, you can leave now."

My boss glared at him, shook his head in disdain, and turned to go. Just then, the door opened abruptly.

It was Interior Minister Gabrovski, who looked shocked at the presence of Belev in Dimitar Peshev's office.

"What are you doing here?" he asked.

"I have a little problem with Mr. Peshev's efforts to derail my operation," Belev said.

"Let's call it what it is," Peshev said. "Killing fifty thousand Bulgarian citizens!"

"You treasonous idiot!" Belev yelled.

"Stop!" Gabrovski stepped between them. "I came here to let Peshev know the news, which you need to hear as well, Belev."

"What's that?"

"The deportations have been halted."

Peshev sighed in relief.

"Impossible!" Belev shouted.

"No, very possible, I'm afraid," Gabrovski replied.

"You did this, you son of a bitch!" Belev shouted, pointing at Peshev. "You'll pay for this *treason*!"

"He was informed by his constituents, Belev," Gabrovski said. "He speaks for them. The question is: How did they know about the March 10 orders in the first place?"

"A rat," Belev snapped.

Gabrovski nodded. "Exactly."

"Church leaders had something to do with it, too."

"Hiding the rats."

"Yes."

As they went back and forth, it was clear that Gabrovski and Belev were of the same ilk. Though different political animals, they both sided with the fascist, anti-Jewish, pro-Nazi faction of the reigning government.

"But who halted it?" Peshev chimed in, seeking clarity on the biggest question. "I mean, I made some colleagues aware. The information was obviously leaked days ago. But who stopped it? Obviously not you, Gabrovski. Not Filov."

All eyes were on Gabrovski.

"The order came from the highest authority in Bulgaria," he said.

"King Boris?"

"Who else?" I said. All three men turned to me. Their condescending stares spoke volumes: *Who told you to speak, woman?*

Judging by their shocked silence, nobody could believe it. As it turned out, the deportation had been called off just hours before midnight. None of the trains—at Dupnitsa, Plovdiv, Kyustendil—would ever leave those stations for death camps in Poland. Thousands of Jews who had been corralled in waiting centers and warehouses throughout the day were sent back to their homes.

And Belev could do nothing about it.

We all exited Mr. Peshev's office. Belev was the last one out, apparently so he could slam the door behind him as hard as possible.

I followed my boss as he stormed through the hallway. On our way out of the building, I heard him mumbling and wasn't sure if he was speaking to me.

"What did you say, sir?" I asked.

"I said, 'Someone is going to *die* for this!'"

"Someone . . . like Peshev?"

"Peshev," he replied, "and the rat."

MARCH 10, 1943

PETER

I could barely sleep that night. Aside from the nightmare of the Cohen family being forced into a cold warehouse and then onto a doomed train, my bed for the night was Ioan's hardwood living room floor. Dad had gone to sleep on the couch next to me, but wasn't there when I woke up. In fact, nobody was around when I first awoke. Then they all came into the room at once—Gancho, Ivan, and Dad, plus Ioan and his wife.

"Have you heard the news, son?"

"No, I just got up."

They were all smiles.

"Look at the newspaper," my uncle said, pushing it in front of my groggy eyes.

One headline read: DEPORTATION OF JEWS STOPPED!

A subheading beneath the fray said: ARCHBISHOP KIRIL HALTS TRAINS IN PLOVDIV.

I looked at my dad with pride, and he gave me a big hug.

We did it! Archbishop Kiril did it! Or maybe Peshev did it. It was more than them, though. It had to be.

"Have you talked to Mom?" I asked.

"She said she had coffee with the Cohens this morning," Dad said. "They are fine. David's back home."

I couldn't believe it. Our little effort from Kyustendil had made a difference.

But after the first minute of elation, I didn't feel as satisfied as I'd imagined.

If things can change so swiftly in one direction, can't they reverse direction just as fast? The fascists are still in power here, still collaborating with the Nazis. As long as that remains true, aren't we all in danger?

LILY

On the morning of March 10, I called in sick.

It wasn't just an excuse. I had a fever and had vomited as soon as I woke up.

I had nightmares of Belev accusing me, attacking me, torturing me; of a shadowy, faceless man putting a gun to Dr. Levi's head and pulling the trigger. In one dream I was drowning in a sealed container filled with water. Somehow, I could hear Belev laughing even though I was struggling underwater. It was as if all the guilt and fear associated with leaking the information had flooded into me all at once.

I couldn't eat. I couldn't even drink coffee.

Most of that morning was spent in bed with the covers pulled over me, as if the blankets would protect me and I could hide there forever.

I cried off and on. Tears of joy for the lives that were saved. Tears of horror at the thought of being caught for my crime.

Fired. Humiliated. Tortured. Jailed.

I am technically a traitor—a spy.

Late that morning, the phone rang.

I assumed it would be Belev, accusing me or maybe informing me of my arrest. And for some odd reason, as I gazed at the black receiver that I was terrified of picking up, I attributed my owning this phone to the good money I made at the Office of Jewish Questions. I could not afford a phone, my clothes, nor my apartment otherwise.

I finally picked up and heard my mother's voice. *Thank God.*

She asked if I could send her more money to pay the bills.

I said, "Yes, of course."

She asked how I was doing and how my job was going.

I said, "Fine."

It was the biggest lie I had ever told her.

MISHO

The drag I took was so big it made me cough harshly.

Smoking cigarettes was still new to me.

I had never smoked early in the morning before. But I couldn't sleep, and I couldn't stop worrying about my mom and sister. My head was spinning long before I'd filled it with smoke.

My insomnia is why I was out in the courtyard so early. Which is why I was the first to see a delivery man at the front gate that morning. He carried a telegram that was folded but not sealed. He said it was for Archbishop Stefan. I told him I would bring it to him immediately. But as I walked up the steps of the main seminary building, I couldn't help peeking. I unfolded the paper and read:

TO: ARCHBISHOP STEFAN (SOFIA)
FROM: ARCHBISHOP KIRIL (PLOVDIV)

THE WORST NIGHTMARE HAS BEEN AVERTED. THE ORDER TO HALT THE DEPORTATION WAS DELIVERED AT THE FINAL HOUR LAST NIGHT. OUR JEWISH CITIZENS WERE ON THE TRAIN STATION PLATFORMS! MY FAITH TELLS ME THAT GOD HAD A HAND IN THIS MIRACLE. BUT I ALSO KNOW YOU DID YOUR PART. THANK YOU, STEFAN. GOD BLESS YOU AND YOUR FLOCK.

OUR JEWISH BROTHERS AND SISTERS HAVE RETURNED TO THEIR HOMES AND CLANDESTINE LOCATIONS UNDER OUR PROTECTION. NOT A SOUL WAS HURT, BUT ONLY SUFFERED THE AGONY OF IMPENDING DOOM. ALL SAFE FOR NOW.

I threw my cigarette on the ground, looked up to the morning sky, and smiled as if my mother and Tatya could see me. Then I ran inside to give Stefan the good news.

PETER

"We've done it," my dad said. "Now we can go back home."

He went into the bathroom to wash up and prepare for the drive to Kyustendil.

Unsettled, but unsure why, I walked out to the narrow balcony and looked down on the city of Sofia. I glared at the swastika banner draped at the entry of a large building across the street.

"Thought it would feel better, huh?" Ioan asked from

behind me.

"Yeah," I said, startled, yet still looking down at the street.

He stepped onto the balcony beside me. "You know why?"

"No."

"Because you're smart enough to know that this war is far from over," he said.

I turned and peered through the windows to see if Ivan or Uncle Gancho were listening to us. I couldn't tell, but part of me didn't care. The journey to Sofia, the fear of discovery, the talk with Peshev—all of it—had made me feel older. I wasn't a kid anymore. And I didn't want to go home and just hope that my family wouldn't become the next victims. I wanted to stay and fight, and somehow Ioan knew it.

"Is there anyone fighting against the Nazis here?" I asked. "Partisans? Rebels?"

"Yeah, but if you're fighting against the Nazis, then you're also fighting against the Bulgarian government that supports them."

"Do you know any rebels?"

"Yeah, they're called the Fatherland Front," Ioan said, lowering his voice as if untrustworthy ears were everywhere. "In fact, I write for them sometimes."

"Write?" I asked.

"They send out pamphlets to inform the people about the need to expel the Nazis and fascists from our country, to organize—then they can begin the socialist revolution."

"Revolution?" I asked. "You mean that Marxist stuff?"

He looked me over, as if surprised at my observation. "That's it, kid."

"I don't know about all that, but I want to kick these Nazis and fascists the hell out of my country."

"Then join the Fatherland Front," Ioan said. "Don't tell your dad I said this, but they need young, brave rebels like you."

"They do? It's that easy?"

"Yeah . . . the hard part will be convincing your father."

Ioan was definitely right about that.

But something inside me pointed at an undeniable truth: I couldn't go back to Kyustendil.

I had to stay in Sofia and fight.

MISHO

After reading the telegram, Stefan gave me a quick hug and told me to get the car.

I asked no questions, and minutes later we were driving up Mount Vistosha's steep winding roads. Stefan had me pull to the side of the road, where a dirt trail ascended into the forest.

"Wait here," he said. "I'm going to pray."

Then he hiked off until he was out of sight. It seemed odd, but then again, it was Stefan.

I waited in the car for a chilly hour, wondering if the archbishop had gotten lost and was freezing to death somewhere on the side of the mountain.

When he finally emerged from the woods, I asked, "Is everything okay, Archbishop?"

"Hardly," he said.

"But my people—my mother and sister—have been saved," I said. "And you helped make it happen."

"Perhaps I assisted," he mumbled.

"Shouldn't we be celebrating?" I asked.

"Misho, sometimes I forget that you are still a boy." Stefan paused to catch his breath. "You're acting as if we've won."

I was confused.

"Haven't we?"

He scratched the center of his beard, then smoothed it down. "Boy, that was only one battle," he said. "This war is far from over."

II

MAY 21, 1943

PETER

I'd been in Sofia for a little over two months, but a lot had changed.

The day I decided I was staying and not returning to Kyustendil with my father and uncle was hell. I'd never had such an argument with my dad. Even though there were others in the room—Ioan, his wife and kids, Ivan, and Uncle Gancho—he yelled at me over and over to obey him. When I refused, his face turned so red and so many veins popped out of his neck that I was afraid he'd have a stroke or a heart attack.

I pleaded my case and argued for my freedom to choose, but he would not listen. The key moment, the one I will never forget, was when he violently grabbed my arm and jerked me toward him. The message was clear: if I didn't cooperate, then he was going to physically force me into the car. I could have submitted, but instead I grabbed his wrist and pushed his arm and body back. His eyes bulged in rage, but I stood my ground, as if to say, "You can hit me, but it's not going to work." His burning eyes turned into a confused, almost empty gaze. I'd disrespected and shamed him in front of everyone in Ioan's living room, and that was it. He'd lost control of me, and he knew it.

"You're going to regret this," he said.

"That's my choice," I said. "I need to stay and fight."

"War is not a game, son," my dad said solemnly. "You'll see."

He left angry, and Ivan followed. Uncle Gancho gave me a silent hug before he departed.

Ever since then, I'd been staying at Ioan's apartment. His wife and kids had moved to the countryside with her parents; with more than one death threat aimed at Ioan, they had decided it was too dangerous for the family to live in downtown Sofia. Ioan could have left with them, but he had tied himself and his purpose too strongly to the Fatherland Front's mission—to eradicate the fascists in power and set up a new socialist government for working people. I grew to understand that he'd downplayed his role at first.

It turned out that Ioan was a true revolutionary Marxist and very courageous. The problem was, for all the revolutionary talk, there hadn't been any action. Sure, we'd go to secret meetings that initially had an air of adventure because they were technically illegal and, if caught, we could be jailed or even killed. But the reality was that we—around fifteen or twenty guys—met once a week in different run-down apartments. The group mostly spouted off about Marxism versus socialism versus communism, or spent hours bashing capitalist imperialism. I would get bored listening because it seemed like these guys were more interested in winning their intellectual arguments than getting out into the world and actually doing something.

Every day, I looked out into the streets and saw Nazi flags flying in my country. I wanted to drive them and their fascist collaborators out, to humiliate them. But I couldn't do it alone. At these Fatherland Front meetings some of the guys had guns, but it seemed like they held them more as validating props than real weapons to use against the enemy.

Yeah, I'd grown frustrated. In over two months, the only thing I had done for our cause was slip anti-fascist leaflets underneath apartment doors with another teen-age FF member named Max. I had done that twice. Only two times! So, at the risk of upsetting my host, I finally told Ioan how I felt about it.

"Well, what are you suggesting, Peter?" he asked.

"I don't know exactly, but some kind of action plan," I said.

"You think going out into the streets and shooting every soldier is going to work?"

"No, that's suicide," I said. "But there's gotta be something. You guys just sit around and talk."

"We're not barbarians," Ioan said. "Plus, Marxist thought is predicated on certain foundations."

"Predi-what?" I said.

"Listen, Peter. Marx told us that 'we have a world to win,' but that the 'workers of the world must unite' first. We can't take action without solid organization."

"What about Marx's saying that 'revolution is the lo-comotive of history'?" I said.

"Ah, you've been listening at the meetings."

"Yeah, but you don't make history just talking about it, sitting on the balcony smoking cigarettes."

Ioan obviously didn't like my tone. He adjusted his collar and spoke with an air of authority. "Peter, when the time is right, we'll strike. And the Front will need you."

"I'm just sick of waiting," I said.

"Have you ever heard the saying 'hurry up and wait'?" Ioan asked. He didn't pause for a response. "Soldiers in the Great War said it because sometimes they would wait at the front for months before there was any action."

"I could *wait* in Kyustendil," I said.

"Your chance to kill Nazis will come soon enough," Ioan said, with a not-so-veiled discomfort at the mention of taking another man's life. "And maybe when it does, you'll wish you were sitting back on this couch, *waiting* instead."

LILY

At the tail end of what had been a long work day, I dozed off at my desk. For over a month I had been on edge, worried that Belev would approach me at any moment and arrest me, attack me, or even shoot me right in the head for being such a traitor. But after weeks of working with Belev in his private office and observing the paperwork that crossed my desk, along with the occasional flirtation, I stopped being afraid of getting caught. For one, I had completely stopped sharing information with Dr. Levi, because there wasn't much to share. But I was also beginning to understand that Belev, far from giving up after the halted deportations in March, was diligently working on an alternative plan. I didn't know much about it yet, but in order to pull it off, he would need to sidestep the entire Parliament and King Boris. Other than that, it was back to secretary work as usual.

"What are you up to?"

The familiar female voice startled me. It was Maggie, my KEV coworker.

"Maggie, you almost caught me falling asleep," I said.

"Sorry, I just came over here to gossip," she said.

"About what?"

Maggie looked around the room as if this gossip was top secret government information.

"Did you hear about Mr. X?"

"Mr. X?" I said. "Are you kidding me?"

"The spy," she whispered.

Suddenly my hair stood on end. I hoped Maggie didn't sense the rush of anxiety that had just shot through every nerve in my body.

"A spy?" I asked with feigned innocence. "What are you talking about, Maggie?"

"Yeah, it's crazy, but I heard they call this spy Mr. X," she said, looking around the room of mostly vacant desks once more to make sure no supervisors were around. "They know information has been leaked from this office, and they suspected this courier that came by the office a lot. Nobody knew his name, so they called him Mr. X. Anyway, he took an important document meant for Prime Minister Filov and gave it to a Jew-loving Parliament member instead, who ended up sharing information with God knows how many people—traitors, if you ask me. So, this Mr. X, they arrested him and put him in an interrogation room, but the man would not confess his crimes—like most damned turncoats, I suppose. When he refused to confess, they actually pulled off his fingernails one by one with pliers."

I winced at the horrific image. "Damn it, Maggie," I said. A cloud of guilt began to smother me.

"I know, it's unthinkable," she said. "But the rat wouldn't even confess after that. So they took a hot iron and branded his feet. Seriously!"

I winced again, but wanted to scream out and muzzle

Maggie into silence.

"Why are you telling me this?"

"Well, he finally confessed," she said.

"He did?" I replied, now wanting more. "And?"

"They executed him," she said matter-of-factly. "Goddamned traitor had it coming."

I stared into Maggie's beady eyes and pondered whether she had come up with this judgment on her own, or had simply heard "goddamned traitor" repeated so many times that it now exited her mouth without a thought.

"Do you believe he—Mr. X—leaked the information?" I asked.

"Jesus, Lily, he *confessed*!"

"After being tortured," I said.

"Still."

"Excuse me!" Belev interrupted our surprisingly tense gossip session, sticking his head out of his office door to address me, Maggie, and the four other people still in the open office space. "I apologize, but this announcement goes for everyone in this room," Belev continued proudly. "There's much to be done before next week so we'll need to work through the weekend. I apologize, but there's essential work and we need you here Saturday and Sunday."

Six tired office workers glanced at each other as if we were accursed, but we all held back any obvious signs of disappointment for fear of upsetting the boss.

"And Lily," he said to me, "come to my office before you leave."

Soon I found myself sitting across from Belev in his private office. He appeared full of energy and extra happy to see me.

"I have good news."

"Splendid," I said, crossing my legs.

"Can I trust you with top secret information?"

I did my best not to squirm out of my seat. "Of course, Mr. Belev." I maintained eye contact.

"Do you remember, months ago, that meeting with Gabrovski and that scumbag Peshev?"

"Yes, I do."

"Well, Peshev has been eliminated," he said.

I held back a gasp at the thought of the Parliament member being murdered.

"He's alive, Lily," Belev clarified, "but he has been silenced by the prime minister after his foolish attempt to have the Parliament sign his pro-Jew petition. The idiot doesn't know a national threat when he sees one. Now, with him out of the way and Parliament in check, our offices can proceed with Plan B."

"I see," I said, and immediately felt pressure to be more enthusiastic. "That's great."

"Would you like to know Plan B?"

"Only if you'd like to share it with me."

"Of course, Lily. You're going to be helping me with the paperwork over the next few days."

"Yes, sir."

"We've come to see the most threatening Jews as the ones who live in Sofia," Belev explained. "They make up the majority of Jews in the country anyway. Next week, without warning, they will be evicted from their homes and transported immediately to the border, where the Germans will move them to camps abroad."

There was the word again—*camps*. He always omitted the word *death*. I guess it made him feel less guilty about the whole thing—if the man was even capable of feeling any guilt.

Belev continued: "Only the military officers who we give orders to will know the procedures and protocol for the mass evictions. And only a handful of officials are privy to this information." He stood up from his desk, hastily put his briefcase in order, and closed and locked it. "And the evictions will be carried out without a snag this time around."

"Sounds like it," I said.

"Do you have any doubts?"

"Well, no," I replied. "But there was talk of King Boris's influence last time."

"Ah, he will not obstruct us," Belev said confidently. "Boris recently had a personal meeting with Adolf Hitler. From what I heard, the Fuhrer made his demands crystal clear."

"Well, then, congratulations," I said.

"For what?"

"For Plan B," I said, doing my best to play an unsuspecting role.

"Thank you," he said, smiling like a mischievous boy who'd gotten away with something.

Belev grabbed two leather holster straps that were hanging on the back of his chair and slipped his arms through the loops. The pistol in the holster was black and looked brand new. He put his jacket on to conceal his weapon.

"Let me walk you out to the street."

"Okay," I said. "You carry a gun now, sir?"

"Indeed," he said proudly. "We're at war, Lily. We have enemies on all sides, especially in this country of idiots."

It was as if Belev had forgotten he was Bulgarian, too.

He walked me downstairs and to the sidewalk on Dundukov Street. He surveyed the area like he was a trained bodyguard.

"It's safe to walk home," he said. "Have a good night, Lily."

"See you tomorrow," I said.

"Oh, yes," he said as though he'd forgotten his weekend work announcement. "Goodbye."

As he said goodbye, he gently held my arm and kissed me on the cheek.

It surprised me—and sent a chill down my spine. But it also gave me confidence. *He is attracted to me, and that alone might help me survive this mess.*

MISHO

Smoking became my habit. Sometimes I hated the taste the nicotine left in my mouth, but I did it anyway. I guess it gave me something else to focus on. As grateful as I was to the archbishop, being trapped inside a monastery got very old and very boring. My people were out there being worked to death in prison camps; millions were fighting and struggling to survive while I was in hiding. I was safe, sure, but there was nothing noble about it. Nothing valiant. Nothing heroic. I stood there smoking in the courtyard like I did every night after dinner, and for the first time in a while, Stefan came out to join me.

"Can you spare one, Misho?"

"Sure," I said. "Smoking again?"

"From time to time," the archbishop replied with a

smile. "Nobody is perfect except for God. Plus, it's been a rough week."

"What happened?" I asked.

"Do you really want to know?"

"I don't know." I exhaled a lungful of smoke. "Do I?"

In a sober tone, Stefan explained some of the political developments. How the anti-deportation Parliament members had been silenced and pushed aside by the pro-Nazi hardliners. How there were rumors that King Boris had been meeting directly with Hitler. How new measures would likely be taken to push Bulgarian troops to the front lines in Russia and remove all Jews from Bulgaria. Ominously, Stefan spoke of the potential need to create more sophisticated basement hideouts for me, the rabbi, and a few others behind the seminary walls.

The news should have frightened me, but I almost welcomed some action. Then I thought of my mother and sister.

"What about my mom and Tatya?" I asked.

"The monastery they're in will take similar measures," he said. "Stricter concealment. They should be safe, though."

Should be.

After the last close call, the archbishop wasn't speaking as confidently about safety for *any* Jews.

But Stefan had been so right about everything else. The halted deportation in March was only one battle. Day after day, the war continued like it would never end. But hadn't King Boris stopped the Nazis' plans before? And didn't Stefan have an influence on the man?

"What about King Boris?" I asked. "Can't he do anything?"

"That's the other bad news, Misho." He inhaled and coughed a bit. "The king spoke to me and the Holy Synod, all the bishops in Bulgaria. He told us something I never expected to hear from his mouth."

Stefan scratched his dark mustache, then ran his fingers down to the gray tip of his beard.

"Well, what did he say?" I asked.

"In effect, he told us to shut the hell up."

"What?" I asked, shocked. "He said that to all the bishops?"

"We must be silent about any measures against Jews. That was his message to all church leaders, but he was mainly speaking to Kiril and I. He resents that we got involved in politics back in March. Now he's hell-bent on keeping us out of it. Out of everything. I asked him to protect at least the converted Jews, and he ignored me. Now he won't even return my calls."

"Why?"

"Because he's afraid of that psychopathic, maniacal windbag—Hitler!" He almost shouted the name. "I'm sure that Boris has been told to let the Nazis decide what's best for Bulgaria."

"Are you going to?" I asked.

"To what?" he said.

"Be silent?"

"Of course not," Stefan proclaimed. "I don't answer to King Boris, I answer to God. And there's no way in hell I'm going to stand idly by while innocent lives are taken."

I nodded in deep admiration of this quirky patriarch of the Orthodox Church.

"Hell?" I repeated his word. "I haven't heard you

curse in a while."

"Some situations call for strong language," he said. Then he sighed and took a step back, signaling that he was about to retire for the night. "And remember, Misho. 'A thousand words will not leave so deep an impression as one deed.'"

Stefan tipped his head at me and began to walk away.

"Is that another Biblical quote?" I asked. "Matthew? Luke?"

The old man chuckled and, without turning around, shouted: "Henrik Ibsen."

I smiled to an empty courtyard—one had to appreciate this atypical archbishop. Though his quote was meant to defend his occasional curse word, I held onto the last two words.

One deed.

One deed could be more significant than a thousand words.

All I wanted was to get out into the world and do at least one deed to make a difference.

MAY 22, 1943

PETER

"Now's the time," Ioan said as he walked into the living room.

"For what?" I asked.

"For what you've been waiting for," he said.

Ioan sat down on the couch across from me and explained that two other Fatherland Front men would be coming over shortly for a meeting, but it wouldn't be a debate about the proletariat and the bourgeoisie. One of the two men, Viktor, had found out the address of the KEV offices, the government agency that enforced Jewish laws and arrest orders. Not only that, but he had the name and picture of the KEV director, Alexander Belev. Ioan handed me the photo, and I focused carefully on the image. Belev had sharp cheekbones and eyes that reminded me of a weasel. This was the man responsible for the deportation and killing of thousands of Jews from Macedonia, and who knew what he was planning next.

When Viktor and his friend, Nikola, joined us, they elaborated on Belev's fascist politics, his collaboration with the Nazis, and his Hitler-esque desire to eliminate all Jews in the country.

"This Belev is a real piece of shit," Ioan said to me.

"Sounds like it," I said. "So, what, are we going to burn the KEV office down?"

"A good inclination, but arson's not our angle," Viktor said.

"It's time to be a true revolutionary," Nikola declared,

glancing at each one of us.

"We're going to kill him?" I asked.

"Assassinate, yes."

"Where? When?"

"In front of his office," Viktor said calmly. "Tomorrow afternoon."

"Wait, tomorrow's a Sunday," Ioan pointed out.

"They're working all weekend," Viktor said. "KEV is trying to push some new policy. That's why we've got to act now."

"Assassination?" I said, the reality setting in.

Ioan could tell I didn't like the sound of it. "Peter, you wanted action. This is it."

Viktor pointed his finger at me and added, "If you crossed paths with Hitler in the street, wouldn't you shoot him?"

"I guess so," I said.

"Well, this guy is Hitler in Bulgaria," Ioan affirmed. "He's responsible for the murder of thousands of innocents."

"And he wants a Nazi fascist government to take over here," Viktor said.

"We have to kill him," Nikola concluded. "He's enemy number one."

Nikola, Ioan, and I listened to Viktor lay out the details of the plan. In all honesty, it was pretty simple. In two pairs, each armed with concealed pistols, we would wait on the opposite side of Dondukov Street the following afternoon. When Belev exited the building alone and unarmed, we would cover our faces with bandanas from the nose down. We would pinch down on him from both sides, at a forty-five-degree angle in order to avoid crossfire. If all four of us fired one shot at the target, there was no way he'd survive.

Once we all fired, we would scatter in four different directions. We figured any witness would be too confused or scared to give chase. And which direction would they go, anyway? With bandanas on, nobody would be able to identify us.

It seemed simple enough. I had questions, but I didn't want to sound like the annoying rookie.

Viktor and Nikola established a meeting point, said they'd bring me a pistol, and left Ioan's apartment. When the door closed behind them, I took in a deep breath, as if I'd been short on oxygen.

"Are you okay?" Ioan asked.

"Yeah," I said. "I just never thought I'd be an assassin."

"Neither did I, but if there's one person to get rid of in this country, it's Belev."

Ioan spoke with full conviction, in the same living room where I'd sat with his wife and kids. He had taken me in like family because he'd recognized my passion to get involved—to do the right thing. But this assassination plan didn't feel right.

"I understand," I said. "It's just that when I pictured fighting in this war, I pictured a fair fight. Both sides armed."

"Wars aren't fair," Ioan said. "The odds against us aren't fair. Most things in life aren't fair, Peter."

"Yeah," I said, not wanting to appear naive.

"And it sure as hell wasn't fair when Belev sent thousands of my people to their deaths."

"You're right," I said.

"And he plans to do it *again*?" Ioan said. "No, he

deserves to die."

Though it didn't sit right with me, I had to agree with Ioan.

Belev deserved to die.

LILY

That Saturday at work, none of my colleagues could have guessed the struggle raging inside of me. There I was, pushing the paperwork forward on Plan B for Jewish eviction orders later the next week. About 20,000 Jews lived in Sofia. That meant 20,000 lives on the line, which was much more horror, grief, and loss than I'd witnessed at the train station in Skopje. It was the whole reason I'd risked my job and my life back in March. Maybe I had helped prevent massive deportations, maybe not. I'd never know, but at least I did my part. My colleagues might call me a traitor if they knew, but millions of others would recognize that saving lives is saving lives. Period.

Sure, I still earned my salary at the KEV office, but that didn't mean I supported the massacre of thousands of human beings—innocent people who were being targeted for their religion, race, and history. Not me.

With a few scattered co-workers in our expansive, desk-filled room and Belev in his private office, I picked up the telephone and called Dr. Levi. I figured it was harmless. I was calling my doctor for a checkup. If he had an opening, I would swing by his office on the way back to my apartment. There was nothing suspect about it.

I waited awhile for the receptionist to pick up—so long, I almost hung up the phone.

"Hello," a female voice finally answered.

"Hi, this is Lily. I'd like to make an appointment for this evening."

"I'm sorry," she said. "Dr. Levi is not available today."

"Will he be in on Monday?" I asked.

"Who is this again?"

"Lily Dimitrova. I was in about two months ago when I—"

"I remember you, Lily," she said and paused. "Dr. Levi is gone."

My heart stopped. *Was he dead?*

"He left the city last month with his family," she told me. "I'm only here to take calls and take notes for clients. We close down officially tomorrow."

I didn't know what to say. "Okay, thank you."

I hung up the phone with a deflated soul. I wanted to alert the Jews in Sofia, but how could I do it without my one contact? Mulling at my desk for an hour, I racked my brain for the answer to this question without having to ask anyone and put myself at further risk of exposure. I was all alone. I had been for months.

After my second coffee in a row, it came to me: the document with the twelve names I saw back in March— the list of supposedly dangerous Jewish men and their addresses in Sofia. The order to arrest them had never been issued because that paper had never left my desk. In the chaos surrounding the halted deportation, and with Belev's sole obsession to correct the deportation failure ever since, the list must have been forgotten.

As discreetly as possible, I scanned the files that had accumulated in the filing cabinets behind my desk. It took me an hour, but I found it. The arrest order from

March 8.

Was this the only copy? Had it been sent out elsewhere? Had it been carried out?

I stared at the first name on the list:

Ioan Goodman, Tsar Simeon 78, 1202.

"Lily!" Belev barked as he approached my desk.

I nearly jumped out of my seat. Not because of anything visibly incriminating, but due to the spy inside me. I didn't attempt to hide the document I held, for fear of appearing conspicuous.

"I know you'd like to leave before dinnertime, but can you please type these papers for me?"

"Of course, sir," I said.

He dropped some freehand notes on the edge of my desk.

"What do you have there?" he asked.

"Just a pile of papers, as usual," I said. "Nothing special."

"I see," he said.

His curiosity seemed to dissipate, thankfully. He turned to go back to his office, but stopped himself.

"And Lily," he said, "you don't need to call me sir. It makes me feel old. Mr. Belev is fine. Perhaps Alexander, if we have the opportunity to meet outside of the office."

"Yes, okay, Mr. Belev," I said and smiled. "I appreciate it."

Meet outside of the office?

Because Goodman was first on the list and his address was only five blocks from my apartment, I headed straight there when I left work. Belev did not escort me out. He was too busy.

I had the two-month-old KEV document folded in

my purse, which could officially be used as evidence of my guilt. On my walk to Goodman's, I rationalized that if anything went wrong, I could just play dumb. Sure, it was a shame that many men treated young women as if they were buffoons, but in this case I would use it to my full advantage.

As I neared his apartment, I wondered if this Jewish man was an actual threat—a criminal who would make me his next victim. What was I walking into? I knew Dr. Levi, but this man was a complete stranger. *He could be untrustworthy. Dangerous.*

When I made it to the street-level front door, I almost turned and walked away. But then I recalled the horror of families being separated at the Skopje train station—the pale stare of that poor condemned woman and her baby. I imagined the next 20,000 being evicted and shipped off to death camps in less than a week.

I labored up four flights of stairs, full of doubts. Then I was knocking on Goodman's apartment door, the fear causing a dizzying nausea, the weight of the moment pressing down.

After waiting for a few seconds, I heard a voice through the crack in the door.

"Who's there?"

"It's Li—" I stopped myself. *Don't give your name.* "I have a message for Ioan Goodman."

PETER

I'd been alone at Ioan's apartment all afternoon, which happened sometimes when he had errands and print work to do. That day it gave me way too much time to think about our plans to murder Belev the next day. It made sense, yet made no sense at the same time. *Will killing him make a difference? Won't the government just replace him? Am I even capable of shooting another human being?*

I'd only shot and killed a bird in the countryside once, and that wasn't a pleasant memory. That day, I proved that I could aim, shoot, and hit a target. And take a life with no particular purpose.

A knock on Ioan's front door startled me.

Nobody ever knocked on his door except grumpy neighbors like Dimo, but that was rare. A few louder knocks made me suspicious. It definitely wasn't the neighbors. *Could it be the police or authorities looking for Ioan?* He was Jewish *and* a member of the Fatherland Front—enough to get him executed on the spot.

I made my way toward the door and waited a while. Finally, I asked, "Who's there?"

"I have a message for Ioan Goodman," a female voice responded.

It was a woman, so I figured it wasn't the police or military.

The tone of her voice was not threatening or authoritative. In fact, she almost sounded like a girl from my high school.

"It's important," she added, with a touch of desperation.

Though it could have been a mistake, I opened the door a few inches to get a look at her.

"Who are you?" I asked.

"Um, Mary," she said awkwardly.

"You're lying," I said. "What's your real name?"

"Is this Ioan Goodman's home? I have a very important message for him."

"Yeah, but he's not here right now," I said. "What's the message?"

"It's confidential."

"Like top secret?" I said, suddenly feeling nervy.

"As a matter of fact, it is," she said. She looked at me as if I were a fool.

"I don't believe you," I said, just to test her will.

"And who am I speaking to?"

"My name's Peter," I said. "I live with Ioan, so you can trust the message with me."

"For some reason I was beginning to trust you," she said, "until you mentioned the word 'trust' and now I'm thinking otherwise."

"Look, I can't tell you when Ioan is coming back," I said, still uncertain whether this girl was a potential threat or not. "But I can tell you that your message will be given directly to him and only him."

She looked my face up and down, so I did the same to her. She was pretty. I hadn't spoken to a girl my age in months. *Is she my age?*

"I'm ready," I said. "Uh, for the message."

"I don't think you are," she doubted. "Are you going to invite me inside or what?"

"Excuse me?" I had gone from skeptical, to cheeky, to attracted, to confused all in less than a minute.

"You're going to need paper and a pencil," she said quite seriously.

"All right," I said and opened the door wider to glance down the hall and make sure there were no soldiers with machine guns waiting to pounce.

She was alone.

"Come in," I said.

LILY

From the moment I laid eyes on him, I could tell this boy, Peter, who answered Ioan Goodman's door, didn't trust me at all.

Frankly, I didn't trust him either.

But if I could get him to relay the message, and Ioan could disperse the information, then my work would be done. When Peter invited me inside, my body tensed as if the situation was an instinctual threat. It was, but I could see he was just a boy—a teenager, younger than me, still in high school. I was his senior and that put me a bit more at ease. He led me into the working-class living room, where I sat down on the well-worn couch.

"Who do you work for?" he asked, as if he were playing a police officer.

"None of your business," I said, swept up by a new wave of confidence. "I don't know you and I'm not about to compromise myself to a teenage boy who I've never met before."

"Are you the one who leaked the information in March?" he asked.

The fact that he knew about *any* leaks took me aback. *Had this become common knowledge—that there was a spy inside the government leaking details about anti-Jewish measures? Were there others besides me, or were my own actions becoming widely known?*

Either way, his question sent a wave of anxiety

through me.

"Look, I'm here to deliver a simple message to Ioan Goodman," I said. "My old contact has left Sofia, and I need to get this information out in order to save lives, do you understand?"

"Save whose lives?" he asked.

"First and foremost, Jews," I said. "Tens of thousands of them. Secondly, the souls of all Bulgarians who would have to live with the knowledge that they stood by and did nothing while Nazis and our own countrymen assisted in the arrest and extermination of every single Jewish person in this nation."

"Wow, so you *are* the one," he said in admiration.

Calling me "the one" frightened the living daylights out of me. I imagined a crosshair target centering on my forehead.

"Ready?" I asked, nodding toward the pencil and notepad on the coffee table. "I want to see you write this down."

He picked up the pencil and paper.

I spoke slowly so he could get every word:

"The Bulgarian government's Plan B: To evict every Jewish resident of Sofia, over 20,000 people, before Friday of next week. They will be told they are moving to work camps, but they are set to be shipped out of the country on trains, delivered to Poland, and imprisoned in death camps. Then all Bulgarian cities will follow the same pattern: Varna, Burgas, Plovdiv, etc. You must alert the Jewish community in Sofia to leave as soon as possible."

PETER

When I'd finished writing down her words, I stared at the attractive young lady sitting on the couch across from me. There I was, a teenager receiving crucial government information from an informant, a spy, but I didn't feel out of place. I didn't feel unready. In fact, I had an urge to jump into action immediately—to do anything possible to stop these unlawful evictions. If they were to be enforced in Sofia in less than a week, then David and my other neighbors in Kyustendil would be next.

"Did you get all of that?" the spy asked.

"Yeah," I said. Then I paused. "But you're telling Jews to *leave town*? Run and hide? That's your solution?"

She stared at me blankly.

"Where are they all going to go?" I asked.

"Anywhere's better than here!" she replied.

"Well, what if we fight back?" I asked.

"Are you crazy?" she said. "And who's *we*?"

"Me. Ioan. The Fatherland Front."

She laughed and raised her eyebrows. "Against the German and Bulgarian armies?" she said. "You have to be kidding."

"You understand that leaving your home voluntarily and being forced to leave amounts to the same thing, right?"

"Hiding somewhere in the countryside versus being sent to your certain death is much different," she snapped.

"I'm just wondering if there's a way to fight this," I said, unwilling to accept being powerless. "You know, show a little bit of courage."

"Kid," she said, "you're confusing courage and insanity."

"Kid?" I replied, offended. "You can't be much older than me. What's your name, anyway?"

"I can't tell you," she said. "My life's already in danger just being here, talking to you. I don't need to make it any worse."

My head was spinning. It didn't make any sense to me. This young woman, whose beauty became more apparent to me by the second, was willing to risk her life by leaking confidential information and going to Jewish residents' apartments, but she wouldn't tell me her real name.

"Then why are you a spy?" I asked.

LILY

The boy was beginning to frustrate me with his questions and his innocence. Plus, I could tell he was attracted to me, which was somewhat repulsive. And the more I sat there in the apartment of this Jewish man—who, along with this boy, looked to be a leader of the Fatherland Front, considered a terrorist organization—the more I had the urge to leave without another word. But when the kid asked me why I was a *spy*, it stunned me.

First of all, I had never heard someone call me a *spy*. That put me in a unique and uncomfortable category. But it was the question "why" that slapped me. I was unprepared—I guess I hadn't put too much thought into it. I'd spent so much time worrying about being discovered and doing my best to not get caught ever since I'd crossed the line, but I'd never talked to anyone about any of my clandestine actions. So here was this teenage boy, throwing the big question at me to answer for the first time out loud.

"Because I've seen things—terrible things," I said, picturing the woman in Skopje. "And I don't want any more innocent lives lost. And I don't want to be associated with—with who I work for."

"Who do you work for?" he asked eagerly.

"You sure ask a lot of questions," I said, annoyed. "I need to go."

I stood up from the couch.

"Okay," he said and awkwardly backpedaled to the front door.

"Please make sure Ioan spreads the word," I reminded him.

"I will, and . . ."

The boy looked at me curiously. I didn't know if he was lonely, naturally awkward, preparing to ask me on a date, or what, but he gazed deeply into my eyes before opening the door.

"Thank you," he said.

"For what?"

"For your courage," he said.

"Maybe it's courage," I told him. "Or maybe the war has made us all lose our sanity."

I slipped through the door and walked away without looking back.

MISHO

I needed to get out.

I didn't really have a plan, but I had to get out into the world and stop living in fear.

Ever since the train of cattle cars with thousands of suffering Jews had passed by me and Stefan near Dupnitsa, I'd been living in fear—constantly worried about myself and my family.

But being trapped inside—aside from the occasional chauffeuring—had gotten old, and hiding had turned shameful. That evening, as the sun set below the freshly green trees, I didn't care if leaving the seminary killed me. I had to get out.

Approaching the southeastern corner of the walled complex, I scanned the area to make sure nobody else was around. In that far, heavily wooded corner, a stack of old firewood made a virtual, if unstable, stairway to the top of the ten-foot-tall brick wall. Stepping up the logs, one at a time, I reached high enough to grab hold of the top edge of the wall and pull myself up.

When my head and shoulders made it above the ledge, I could see a mostly empty road with two army jeeps approaching. As they drove nearer, I spotted swastika symbols on the side of the vehicles, and instinct told me to duck. The problem was, the sudden shift put most of my weight on my feet, which were lightly balanced on top of the precarious wood stack. My movement kicked one of the logs out from under my feet, sending me flailing back into the yard along with some of the loose, bark-encrusted wood. Scraping against some logs on the way down, my body hit the dirt with a dull thud. At that moment, I wasn't sure if the pain was physical or more from the embarrassment of complete failure.

I heard a distressed voice.

"Are you okay, son?"

It was Stefan, who hurried over to me and knelt down. "What in the name of Mary and Joseph happened?"

"I don't know," I said, groaning in pain.

"Were you trying to leave? Have you lost your mind?"

I sat up, checking the cuts and scrapes on my hands and knees. I didn't say anything, afraid that if I did I might start to cry.

"Misho, I've gone to great lengths to keep you safe here," Stefan said. "Your situation is privileged. You can't just throw it away!"

Stefan looked deeply into my eyes as if he could read them.

"Answer me. Were you trying to leave?"

It was difficult to explain. *Did I want to get out for a few hours and come back? Or did I want to leave for good and reunite with my mother and sister? Or truly rebel and join a resistance group to fight back?*

"I'm tired of hiding," I said. "I feel . . . ashamed."

"Ashamed?" he yelled. "Of what—surviving? Being alive rather than dead?"

"It's just that—" I started to speak and then stopped, unsure of myself. Unsure of everything.

"Spit it out," Stefan urged.

"I want to do something," I said. "*Anything*. If that means fighting for my people, then I'll fight."

"Oh, Misho," he said. "That would be like an animal telling Noah that he'd rather take on the flood by himself. 'Thanks for the invite onto your boat, but I'll go it alone!' It's ludicrous!"

"Well, if you put it that way it makes me sound really stupid," I admitted.

"Exactly, but you're not stupid," Stefan told me. "You had an impulse to leave, sure, but you didn't think it through."

"I'm thankful, Archbishop, I am. It's only that . . ."

"You don't want to live in fear," he said. "I understand that nobody wants to live like that, Misho. But we are in an extenuating circumstance—a true crisis. Hundreds of thousands of lives, maybe millions, are at stake. What's more, our souls are at stake."

I didn't know what he meant by that, so I stuck to my simple truth.

"I don't want to sit here and do nothing while my people are dying," I said.

"Valiant, Misho, but there are other ways to resist," Stefan said. "Have you ever heard the saying 'The pen is mightier than the sword'?"

"Yes, but . . ." I recalled my recent conversation with the archbishop. "You always talk about doing deeds—acts rather than faith."

"That was in a different context," he said and stood up from his crouching position. "You can't take one quote and apply it to everything, Misho."

What? I was confused. Humiliated. My hands, knees, and neck were in pain. This old monk didn't understand me and my people's struggle. Our will to fight against the Goliaths of the world. My readiness to act in the face of Hitler's evil. But, as I picked myself up off the ground and Stefan brushed the dirt off my arms and back, I couldn't say anything to him.

Because, so far, he had saved my life.

"You'll have your moment to act, Misho. But today is not the day. Trust me."

Stefan patted me on the back and guided me onto the paved walking path.

"Now is a particularly dangerous time for Jews here," he said as we ambled along.

Why? But I didn't ask the question out loud. I didn't need to.

"The government's initial plan to evict and massacre all Jews failed in March. Now those in charge want to please their Nazi bosses by making sure it happens this time without obstruction. There have been a few raids on Jewish homes in Sofia recently. Rumor has it that all Jews in the capital will be evicted by soldiers within a week. The rest of Bulgaria will follow suit."

"How do you know?

"I received a phone call about thirty minutes ago. There's someone leaking information from the Jewish Commissariat intelligence offices."

"A spy?" I asked.

"Something like that."

I pictured the spy at work, stealthily hiding top secret documents in a briefcase and risking his *life* to save us. And he wasn't even Jewish! How could he be—or she? No, it had to be a he. In wistful admiration of this mystery hero, I gazed at the orange glow made by the sunset in the distance.

"So we need to act fast," Stefan said.

"We?" I said.

"On Monday I will be giving a speech at Nevski Cathedral. It's supposed to be on St. Cyril and Methodius, but I have other plans." Stefan paused before continuing gravely. "I must speak of the great peril Jewish families are facing from the fascists in power. I'll deliver a message to the government and all Christians to support and protect our Jewish friends and neighbors however we can. It's the least I can do."

"Won't that put you in great danger?" I asked.

"I'm already in danger, Misho," he said with a smirk. "I'm harboring Jews. Regardless, it's the right thing to do."

Respect for the quirky, saintly man welled inside me.

"And it's God's will," he added.

Honestly, I hadn't thought about God lately. The last time I had, it was to question his existence. *How could a loving creator allow his people to be killed by the thousands? What kind of God is that?*

"Am I driving you there?" I asked.

"Yes, and standing by my side," he said. "God willing."

"Of course," I answered.

We stopped short of the gravel driveway that led to my spartan quarters.

"Now wash your wounds and get some sleep," he said. "You must be ready for Monday."

MAY 23, 1943

MISHO

In my dream, I was standing at the rear of the stage while the archbishop delivered a sermon to thousands in front of Nevski Cathedral. As he spoke into the microphone and the crowd stood eerily quiet, I peered around the square and caught sight of a man in black crouched on the balcony of a nearby apartment. I could see that he held a rifle, and was aiming it at Stefan, center stage. Before my feet could move, or my mouth could produce a sound, a single shot rang out. I looked up and the assassin was already gone.

I moved in slow motion to Stefan's fallen body. The bullet had struck him in the center of his chest, but with his dark robes on, the wound was barely visible. Blood soon pooled out underneath him. Others huddled around Stefan, but he focused on me. His words were labored, delivered with his last breath, but they were clear as day.

"Do what you must, Misho."

Then he expired.

A woman screamed offstage and I turned to see who it was.

She was a blonde young woman wearing a red coat.

When I turned back to Stefan, he was gone. Then everyone was gone. I was kneeling on the stage completely alone.

That's when I woke up sweating, panting, my heart pounding.

The nightmare stuck with me all day.

PETER

I hadn't slept much. The night before, Ioan had me running around Sofia, knocking on doors, spreading the word that evictions were happening soon. By morning, the spy, Ioan, and my own efforts had turned into hundreds of telephone calls and a community plan: to take to the streets on Monday in protest of the government's eviction plans and to demand that Jewish lives and property be protected. It was bold because it would rely on the goodwill and support of more politicians like Peshev—who had since been removed from office. At best, the demonstration would delay the evictions and put pressure on the Parliament to do the right thing. At worst, police and the military would see a massive crowd of Jews and their supporters all gathered in one place and decide to massacre them in the streets.

So much had happened in the past twenty-four hours that when there was a knock on Ioan's door, I had no idea who it might be—friend or foe. I opened the door to see Viktor and Nikola's faces.

Jesus, it was Sunday. *The day.*

"*Dobro utro*," Viktor said and shuffled in, followed by Nikola.

They both plopped down on the living room sofa as if they owned the place. Ioan entered the room with his third coffee in his hand and sat down.

I remained standing, wondering if the plan was still solid.

Nikola pulled out his pack of cigarettes and distributed them to all, but I declined. Soon the room was so full of smoke that I might as well have smoked my own.

"We'll need to wait outside the KEV office from noon on," Viktor said. "We might catch him going to lunch, or leaving work in the afternoon."

"What if he's with someone?" Ioan asked.

"I've been watching," Nikola said. "He's usually alone, or with a girl."

"With a child?" I asked.

"No, like a young woman," Nick explained. "A secretary or something."

"What if she's in the way?" Ioan said. "I'm not killing a secretary!"

"Or what if he's with a guy—like a soldier as his guard?" I asked.

Viktor sighed in exasperation, as if his plan was being uprooted. "Look, there are four of us."

"Three," Nikola said. "I'm supplying the guns—which were not cheap—and on lookout for you guys."

"Okay, there's three of us," Viktor said. "That's two more than we need for one Nazi asshole who isn't expecting anything and walks down Dundukov Street like he's the king of the Balkans. We have the element of surprise. We have the arms."

"What if there's two or three of them?" I asked.

"Christ, if Belev is surrounded by the Thirty-Eighth Battalion, then we wait for another day. But if he's solo or even with a co-worker, we take the opportunity."

It still didn't feel right. I didn't want to be an assassin, and I sensed that these guys were amateurs, too. Then, as if on cue, Nikola placed the three handguns on Ioan's coffee table as if he'd never touched a weapon before. Two pocket pistols and a .38 revolver lay there.

Ioan looked me in the eye. "Here's the action you

wanted, Peter."

I nodded but didn't agree.

"What about the demonstrations tomorrow?" I said. "They might work, and then killing Belev wouldn't be necessary."

"What are you saying, kid?" Viktor asked.

"I don't know. Why not wait until after the demonstration tomorrow? If it doesn't work, then we kill Belev."

"Doesn't work like that," Ioan said. "This is about ending fascism."

"We've been waiting a long time for intel like this," Nikola added.

"Intel?" I blurted out. "Are you kidding? You've watched this guy leave work a few times while you snack on *banitsa*!"

Ioan cracked a smile, but Viktor scowled at my defiance.

"Hey, what's this kid's problem? Maybe his allegiance is elsewhere."

The room went silent.

Now my loyalty is being called into question? If I had to pick a side, there was no question that I was on the right one.

"Belev is still Belev," Ioan said to me. "His job is to exterminate Jews in this country. He's handing our nation over to Hitler. That won't stop because of a protest in the streets tomorrow."

"Bottom line," Viktor added matter-of-factly, "killing Belev does the country a favor. He deserves it."

Nikola and Ioan nodded with certainty.

"Now are you in or out?"

I imagined David being evicted, bludgeoned on the

head, dragged out of his home in my own neighborhood.

"Yeah, I'm in," I said.

LILY

I teetered between death and redemption.

That Sunday in the office was especially difficult.

As I swayed between the mindless task of filing paperwork and the gravity of being caught for my crimes and sentenced to death, a disturbing truth emerged.

We were in the office rushing things along on a weekend because the evictions were to begin the next day—Monday morning! I had risked my job and life to tell Ioan's young friend about the evictions, but it was too late. They really had only one day. It chopped my sense of purpose like a butcher knife on a cutting board—the reality of knowing that, while the risks were high, the rewards were mostly unknown.

What was I doing? What was I fighting for?

My mind raced back and forth until Belev approached my desk that afternoon. I imagined him asking me questions and me folding like a worn rag doll; then being shot in the back of the head, or hanged, or thrown off the cliffs of Kaliakra. Every terrible form of death flooded through my mind until I arrived at my own pleading, fear-stricken bargain.

My work saving Jewish lives is done. No more risks. I'm not a real spy.

I had done what I could. I'd atoned for Skopje and my job at the KEV. I would forget every treasonous thing I had done—throw those memories in the incinerator.

Move forward and let Belev know that my loyalty was with him. Yes, it was the only way to survive.

"Lily!" Belev snapped me out of it. "Are you okay?

"Sorry, what?"

"I've been standing here for a few seconds."

"I apologize sir, I guess I was just—daydreaming."

"No time to daydream in this office," he said. "We have these files that need to be processed by four o'clock. Can I trust you to get them finished?"

"Yes, of course, sir."

"I'd like to walk you home today, but I have to run something over to the Parliament building and you have a mountain of work."

"Yes, I do." I sighed, overwhelmed.

He paused and looked me over.

"Actually, do you want to take a short break? Walk with me?"

In spite of an odd pressure to please him, I nervously settled on professionalism and avoidance.

"Thank you, sir, but I have to finish my work."

"All right. I appreciate your loyalty, Lily."

PETER

For the passersby on Dundukov Street, it was just another afternoon. For me, it was either the beginning or the end. If I killed a man, there would be no going back. I'd be a murderer or an assassin, for better or worse, for the rest of my life. Or, if something went horribly wrong, I could wind up dead or in jail—thus the *end* of my life.

Since Nikola knew Belev's face and had been casing

the building for days, he waited by the entrance unarmed. The plan had evolved a little bit. When Belev emerged, Nikola would take off his fedora hat and briskly walk away. That was the *go* signal. But because Nikola had no idea when Belev would leave the building, he simply waited there, leaning against parked cars and smoking a full pack of cigarettes while Viktor, Ioan, and I nervously waited with pistols in our pockets, spaced out on the opposite side of the street.

What must have been just over an hour seemed like an eternity. At first, I incessantly touched the metal handle of the gun inside my pocket just to make sure it was still there, but then I stopped, almost wanting to forget that I planned to use that gun in broad daylight. We were banking on shooting Belev without a hitch, running in opposite directions, and never being identified—all on the clearest sunny day you can imagine. As we lingered and surveyed the area, I noticed that as many as ten people could be walking on each side of the street at any given time. That made twenty potential witnesses!

That and every other bad thought crossed my mind in the time that we waited. Like a nervous twitch, I would glance twelve meters down the sidewalk at Ioan, and Ioan at Viktor another twelve meters further away, and Viktor back to me. Then we'd all return our focus to Nikola's hat, expecting it to be pulled off at any time.

When his hat actually came off, my perception of time became dreamlike. Nikola walked away so fast, he might as well have sprinted. Belev emerged onto the sidewalk with a man by his side—or was it the other way around? Which one was Belev? Both men had on smart suits and resembled each other—they could have been

Aryan brothers.

I looked at Viktor and he jerked his head in Belev's direction, indicating for us to move in. We crossed the empty street and would have been run over if any car had driven by, due to our laser focus on the two Nazis. It was the closest to true tunnel vision I've ever experienced. With my stomach twisted in knots and adrenaline pumping, I glanced around for guidance and saw that Ioan had already pulled out his pistol and pointed it toward the two men. He fired a shot at Belev from the middle of the street and missed. As Viktor pulled out his weapon, so did Belev and the man with him.

Me? I froze as the shootout unfolded in slow motion—all four seconds of it.

Because Ioan and Viktor got Belev's attention first, I was on the periphery, practically behind Belev's line of sight, separated by a parked DeSoto. Hunched behind the big car, I watched as Ioan took his second shot and missed again. Belev, unfazed, returned a slug into Ioan's chest. Viktor fired at Belev's right-hand man, who shot back and put Viktor on the pavement, writhing in pain. Still behind the DeSoto, I watched Ioan fall to his knees on the hard cobblestone street. He looked at me in shock and despair as he gasped his last breath. Further down the street, Viktor whined grotesquely. If I didn't run now, I would be shot while crouching behind this car, or arrested, in the next few seconds. Not wasting another moment, I darted away with my head down.

A few strides in, a bullet whizzed past my head. Moving faster than ever before, imagining Belev pointing his gun at my back, I dashed laterally on every second stride. Another bullet whizzed by me. Soon I was around the corner and running to the next street. I turned right, then left, zig-zagging my way through so many blocks I lost count. Finally I ducked behind a bush in a park and tried to catch my breath, as if I had forgotten to breathe while running. My legs went noodley, and I went down to my knees.

What the hell had just happened back there?

Ioan was dead. Maybe Viktor, too.

Belev had definitely survived. And he had probably been the one shooting at me.

My hand went into my pocket to feel the cool metal of the pistol. My body froze in shock, incapacitated, as if all my joints had locked up.

I'd never even pulled out my gun.

I had completely failed.

LILY

I only witnessed the tail end of it.

When I heard the first shot, I immediately knew Belev was involved. He'd just left the office with Boyko and—*damn, it could have been me with him*!

Unlike the others in the office, that first gunshot drew me to the closest window overlooking Dundukov Street. It was foolish of me, sticking my head into plain view of a gun battle, but I wasn't thinking. I saw Belev shoot one attacker dead in the street. The man fell to his knees and crumbled onto the ground. It looked like Boyko shot the other terrorist, but it could have been Belev. From my elevated vantage point, I noticed another man hiding behind a large black car parked along the sidewalk, blocking him from Belev's view. The angle was poor, but I caught a glimpse of the man before he ran from the scene like an Olympic sprinter. Belev shot at him twice, but missed, yelling in frustration as the man fled the scene.

Was it a boy? Was it—no, it couldn't have been . . .

The would-be assailant who ran away looked exactly like the teenage boy I had spoken to in Ioan Goodman's apartment, the one who was part of the Fatherland Front, a group that would likely target Belev.

Was it him?

Belev barged into our open office space.

"Those goddamn Commies tried to kill me!" he said, out of breath. "Lily, call an ambulance for Boyko."

Frantic, I ran to the phone and dialed the hospital.

"Did you see anything?" Belev asked.

"What?" I said.

"The attackers? The one who ran away? Did you see his face?"

"Um . . . no, it happened too fast," I said.

Listening to each ring, I waited for the hospital operator to pick up.

Belev could have been shot by the teenage boy—Peter. Christ, I knew his name. If it was even him.

At that moment, I didn't want to know either of them. But I also didn't want anyone else to die. I wanted the war to be over and to be back in my normal life.

"Hello, Aleksandrovska Hospital operator."

"There's been a shooting in the street," I said, hearing my own voice half-muted, as if it were not mine. "Dundukov Street. Three men have been shot. Hurry!"

Belev tied a cloth tightly over Boyko's bleeding

wound and turned to me.

"You didn't see anything at all, Lily?"

"Only a boy—a man—running away. That's all."

"A dirty Jew, I have no doubt," he said, still out of breath. "I'll have every police officer scour the city for the cowardly little shit."

My insides dropped into suspended animation. *Was I afraid for Peter's life, or my own?*

I repeated to myself over and over: *I didn't see anything. I don't know anything.*

MISHO

Captivity. I had done nothing all day except read, walk through the yard, eat, and worry. I watched the sun fall below the horizon, which for me was the top of the western seminary wall. And I couldn't get that nightmarish vision out of my head—of the archbishop being shot, lying lifeless on the stage.

As usual, before dinner I smoked a cigarette in the courtyard by myself.

"That's deadly," a voice said.

I turned, startled. It was Rabbi Zion.

Could he read my mind?

"What?" I said.

"Smoking," he said casually. "It will kill you."

"How do you know?"

"They mass-produce cigarettes," he said. "How do they make them? Processed in a factory in some unnatural way, of course. Can't be good for you—to inhale something so antithetical to oxygen."

"I'm okay so far."

"So far," he repeated, and paused. "Is something troubling you today, young man?"

"Something has troubled me every day this year," I admitted.

"Isn't that the truth," the rabbi muttered, wiping his furrowed forehead. "I mean, specifically. I saw you walking in the yard today, and you obviously carry a burden."

I inhaled an antithetical cloud, unwilling to open up. But I had nobody else to talk to and there was no harm in sharing with the rabbi, who was also stuck hiding behind these walls.

"I had a bad dream last night that I was at tomorrow's speech with Stefan and an assassin shot him and he fell down on his back."

"I see."

"It was all very real . . . too real," I said. "I want to warn him."

"You can't do that, Misho," the rabbi said.

"Why not? It's for his safety."

"First of all, it was only a dream. Secondly, there's nothing you can say that will stop him. Archbishop Stefan is an extraordinary man."

"I know that, but—"

"I mean, he's not ordinary. Not normal." There was a hint of envy in the rabbi's voice. "He fears nobody—truly nothing but God. It's very rare."

"Are you saying it's okay if he dies tomorrow?"

"No, of course not! I'm saying that he, unlike so many of us, will stand up for what is morally right, regardless of the powerful forces facing him. And he takes his position with this phrase in mind: 'Thy kingdom come, thy will be done.' In essence, if he dies carrying out God's will, then he's fine with it. There are few human beings who have such courage."

It sounded as if the rabbi was rubber-stamping Stefan's execution. It perplexed me.

"So if you somehow knew Stefan would be shot, you wouldn't try to stop it?" I asked.

"Keep in mind, dreams are dreams. They tell you next to nothing aside from your own fears." He seemed to ponder for a moment. "Again, you or I could say anything to Stefan, but ultimately he will only listen to God. And if God tells him that he must do and say everything in his power to stop the mistreatment of Jews, then he will."

"So you're saying he wants to become a martyr?"

"I'm saying that true martyrs are rare, and when they become martyrs it's not because they want to. They are called by a higher power. They *have* to."

I shook my head as I again envisioned Stefan being harmed.

"You are lucky to know a man like the archbishop," Rabbi Zion added.

That much I already knew, which was why I couldn't bear the thought of driving him to his death the next morning.

MAY 24, 1943

PETER

Ioan was dead.

It didn't seem real to me. Nothing did.

I'd spent the night hiding in the storage space underneath the staircase of an unknown apartment building, about a kilometer away from the shooting. I'd spotted a police officer on the street and sneaked inside, opting to share a dark, dingy closet with cockroaches and spiders. Anything other than capture, imprisonment, and execution was fine with me.

The next morning, after an hour of willing myself to go outside, I walked straight to Nikola's apartment.

When he opened the door, he just stared at me for a few seconds. Part of me wanted to blame him for the failure of our mission; the other part wanted to hug him for still being alive.

I did neither.

"What happened?" he asked.

I shook my head. "Ioan is dead. Victor was shot. I don't know—"

"Victor's alive. He was arrested." There was fear in Nikola's quivering voice.

"What's the next move?" I asked.

"There is no next move."

"Ioan's death will not be for nothing," I said.

Nikola sighed as if defeated, then suddenly sparked to life. "There's a demonstration planned later today because of the orders to evict Jews," he said. "They're protesting. There's also a Cyril and Methodius Day event in front of Nevski today. Lots of people will be in the streets."

"Sounds like the perfect setting for a revolution," I said.

"It sounds like suicide to me," he said.

For me, it was the moment that Karl Marx had talked about. The people were standing up and taking to the streets because conditions had only worsened. There was nothing to lose. If this was an opportunity to make change and shift the tides, then I would take it.

"Do you have that list of Front phone numbers?" I asked.

"Yeah, but—"

"Give it to me. I need to make some calls."

I called over a hundred numbers. Some did not answer, but most did. My message was simple: *If you want to be a part of the change we need, then be at Nevski Cathedral at noon today.*

I didn't know what I was doing, but at least I was doing something.

MISHO

In the seminary driveway, I sat behind the wheel of the idling car as Stefan approached in his usual dark robes, silver crucifix around his thick neck. He opened the door and said good morning to me like it was any other day.

As I inched forward on the gravel, Rabbi Zion rushed up to the passenger side and knocked on the window. I rolled it down.

"It's already started, Stefan."

"What?"

"The evictions have begun!" the rabbi said. "I just got the news. Hundreds, maybe thousands of Jews are marching today in the city center in protest. It will not be safe."

The rabbi glanced at me, surely recalling our conversation and my premonition. Perhaps his sleep had been plagued by his own nightmares.

"Thank you for the warning," Stefan said. "What time, and where?"

"Stamboliyski," the rabbi gasped. "They'll be gathering there en masse."

"Good. The people are standing up. Perhaps I will mention this in my speech."

"But Archbishop, it's too risky!" the rabbi pleaded through the car window. "Didn't the king warn *you* specifically to stay out of politics?"

"Rabbi, this isn't a political issue, it's a human issue."

The rabbi paused and took in the moment, the morning air. "I'm coming with you then," he declared unexpectedly.

"But, Rabbi Zion, you just explained the dangers!" Stefan said.

"And it didn't stop you, Archbishop."

The rabbi slipped into the back seat and patted me on the right shoulder as if to say it was okay to go now—despite what he'd said to me the day before, despite my nightmares.

When we hit the cobblestone streets of downtown Sofia, Stefan had still not said a word to me. The rabbi was silent now, too. We were quickly nearing Nevski

Cathedral. I had to say something to the archbishop.

"I'm worried about you today," I said.

"Nothing to worry about," he said. "You just stand by the stage and you'll be fine. God will be with us."

"Yes, with God's help, we'll be fine," the rabbi added.

"But you're speaking publicly, against government orders, in the middle of a war," I said.

"*Me?*" Stefan said. "Don't worry about me, Misho. I've been taught to tell the truth, no matter what. Especially if there's injustice, you have to speak up."

Police had cordoned off an area for us to park on the north side of the cathedral, near the Parliament building. That symbol of the government, right next to the golden-domed symbol of the Church, made the clash between the two seem more inevitable.

Stefan versus King Boris.

Stefan versus Gabrovski.

Stefan versus Hitler.

And now he would stand before everyone, speaking to the audience already massing in front of the stage set up especially for this day.

I opened the car door for Stefan and asked, "Are you sure about this?"

"The Gospel According to Matthew says that being a rock of the church, one of many, is the key to the kingdom of heaven. I'll do my best to be a rock today, Misho."

If only he was an actual rock; then he could deflect bullets.

The crowd was easily a few thousand strong, all standing in front of the stage at the entrance to the cathedral. We three waited off to the side of the shoulder-high platform while a priest warmed up the crowd. I couldn't help but peek out and scan the balconies that looked over the square. Many people stood on their terraces and watched, but nobody like in my dream. Nobody with a rifle in their hand.

I scanned the many faces with both fear and interest. The energy of the crowd heightened my sensations—after all, I had not been outside the seminary walls for weeks. I had not seen so many people gathered together in years!

As that thought crossed my mind, I saw her.

The young blonde woman stood to the left side of the stage looking out, a bit of space between her and the dense pack closer to the stage. It was not only her beauty that caught me, but also her expression. Was it concern? Fear? Confusion? Her eyes darted around as if she were looking for someone.

What made her memorable—and my mental image of her is as clear as if it were yesterday—was that she wore a scarlet-red coat. Not only did the color stand out, but it was almost summertime and the weather was warm. Why a coat on a hot day? It didn't make sense, but it made her more intriguing, more mysterious—maybe even suspicious.

And then I felt my heart stop beating.

A woman in a red coat had been in my dream.

LILY

On the way to work, I noticed a crowd gathered in front of Nevski Cathedral and recalled that it was Cyril and

Methodius Day—a national holiday that the pro-Nazi government didn't recognize. It hadn't occurred to me because the main thing on my mind were the evictions of Jews that had started that morning. Another question that concerned me was whether or not the boy, Peter, had survived the night.

Is he in custody? On the run?

Am I the only witness who can identify him?

Should I identify him to the police to erase any suspicion against me?

The crowd cheered as Metropolitan Stefan took center stage. I should have continued walking to work, but something kept my feet planted in place, anticipating something more than a typical sermon. I had heard of the archbishop in passing. The stout, bearded holy man was eccentric and considered liberal for a church patriarch.

First he spoke about Cyril and Methodius's contributions to Christianity and their creation of the Cyrillic alphabet, but it quickly turned political. He said these two revered apostles would certainly disapprove of the "pogrom being waged against the Jews." He spoke of the need for "humanity and brotherly love" in protecting the Jews within our borders, saying that Bulgarians were tolerant and respected freedom, and that the Church should protect minorities from the tyranny of the majority. He proclaimed that he would "baptize all Jews as Christians that day" if it would save them from "deportation and certain death." He told the silent audience that it was time "the ship of state put aside all exclusionary, discriminatory, and oppressive policies."

This was already a radical speech for a priest, or anyone at the time—something worthy of harsh consequences, no doubt—but then the archbishop started to name *names*! He called out Filov, Gabrovski, and King Boris for being guilty of bowing to the demands and influence of foreign control—to the Nazis, to Adolf Hitler! He preached the truth right there in front of thousands, and the majority cheered in agreement.

Archbishop Stefan was so right, it scared me. As I watched the holy man make the sign of the cross and leave the stage, I sensed the extreme danger he was in, which reminded me of the danger I also faced. *Every day.* My eyes followed Stefan all the way offstage, afraid he would be shot on the way, or swiftly tackled by the authorities and arrested. When he was safely out of sight, I pivoted to walk to work. Then I heard someone shouting, "*Sloo-shai-te, vsichki!*"

I turned to see who the speaker was and froze.

It was Peter. The boy from Ioan Goodman's apartment.

He was the attempted assassin! Now I was sure of it.

He stood up boldly on a bench no more than twenty meters from me, gathering the vast crowd's attention on his own, repeating: "Everyone, listen up!"

PETER

There were more than I imagined. Maybe thousands.

The largest group I had ever spoken to was my high school classroom of twenty kids in Kyustendil. That had been about a year before, which now seemed a lifetime ago.

After a few seconds of standing on a bench and

yelling like a madman, I had the crowd's attention. I sensed I wouldn't have it for long, so I got straight to the point.

I told them that Metropolitan Stefan was right. That we Bulgarians were not depraved like the Nazis. That we would not let them kill Jewish citizens of our state, because if that happened, we wouldn't have much of a state to claim or be proud of in the future. But that we shouldn't rely on the Church to save Jews—we, the people, should stand up and protect them! My vocal chords burned as I told the crowd that government officers were evicting Jewish people from their homes at that very moment, and moving them to detention camps; that many were currently gathered in front of the synagogue on Maria Luisa Boulevard to demonstrate against this injustice.

"Let's join them now!" I yelled, then paused to catch my breath.

I heard murmurs throughout the crowd, but most eyes remain locked on me. Scanning the faces, I saw both hope and fear.

Then I shouted, "Are we merely slaves of the Nazis who are in control of our government? Let's march to the center and join our Jewish neighbors in defiance of foreign domination! We have nothing to lose but our chains!"

A few shouts of "*Haide!*" echoed through the crowd. And then more. "*Haide!*" "*Haide!*" "*Come on!*" "*Let's go!*"

I jumped off the bench and led the way toward the synagogue. At first, I didn't want to turn around for fear that nobody would be following me, but when I finally did turn back there were hundreds behind me. Maybe thousands.

MISHO

My eyes were locked on the crowd after the teenage boy's rallying cry from atop a park bench. It was a distinct call to action—a moment in life where you have to make a choice. It was my chance to support my people in the midst of a war stacked against us.

All of us.

Turning back to the archbishop, I saw that he was preoccupied, speaking to men in suits. I would find out later that one of the suits was none other than Prime Minister Filov.

The important thing was that Stefan was off the stage, had not been shot by an assassin, and was distracted.

As half the people began to move in the direction of the teenage speaker, it was less my decision and more like gravity had shifted and pulled me into the crowd with them. I scanned back to see if the young woman in the red coat was still there.

She was—squinting at the mass of people as if confused, or in need of corrective lenses. I waded through the thick crowd to get closer to her. When our eyes met from a few meters away, I stopped.

She was more attractive close-up, even though she didn't smile at me in the slightest. Still, my heart raced and I forgot how to breathe. Like an idiot, I put my hand out toward her even though she was too far away to grab it.

I turned it into a waving gesture toward me, as if to say, "Come on." Then I smiled and said it out loud to her: "*Haide!*"

LILY

No, no, no!

I looked at this skinny, dark-haired boy's desperation, part of me really wanting to join him in the march.

Why? Because they were right. Metropolitan Stefan and Peter were right. It's why I had risked my job and my life in the first place—to save Jewish people from not only grave injustices, but death. To save the rest of us from a terrible sin.

But since the assassination attempt on Belev, something inside me had shifted and taken over. Fear had consumed me and convinced me to lock all of my spying secrets into a compartment deep inside myself and forget about them. Bury them. Save myself.

This is the only thing that can save me.

The fear of my own death had turned me into something else. I can't say that I'm proud of it, but it was a matter of survival.

Still standing there, the desperate teenage boy in the crowd said it again: "*Haide.*"

To join the demonstration would be to commit suicide, which I had already come close enough to in my risky endeavors. Plus, Belev had been on edge lately, and I needed my job and income to support my parents.

I shook my head no, and walked away toward Dundukov Street. The truth was, I was scared to death about *everything*.

Fear consumed every bone in my body. And I desperately wanted to change that.

PETER

The ten minutes it took to lead the crowd from Nevski Cathedral to the synagogue on Maria Luisa Boulevard might have been the best ten minutes of my life. Though I walked alone, I heard the voices of those behind me. Their words were filled with anger at the injustice and the low point our country had hit, but the collective energy and sound of our footsteps gave me hope.

Hope that people united could actually do something.

Maybe Marx was right about the working class forging a genuine revolution?

Maybe we could put so much pressure on the government that we could actually oust the fascists in power!

We reached the street in front of the synagogue, and the faces there—many of them Jewish—first looked at us in shock and fear. They were apprehensive. I yelled, "*Nie sme solidarni s vas!*" *We are in solidarity with you!*

And they cheered.

With the momentum of our massive crowd joining the large Jewish group already amassed, we took over the street and marched south toward Sveta Nedelya Church in the center.

No longer in front, I became engulfed by the crowd. My main purpose, to organize and bring people together to support Jewish lives, had been fulfilled. But as we pushed forward, I realized that the outcome was completely out of my hands. In fact, the sense of control I had held only ten minutes before had completely vanished. Now I was a minnow in the middle of a school of fish going downriver, with a strong current pushing from behind.

I craned my neck and jumped to see over the crowd, but it was no use.

I could not see what was in front of us.

MISHO

It was a rush, all of it.

Moving with the crowd toward the synagogue, I quickly forgot about the woman in the red coat who had just rejected me. Her mysterious connection to my dream and her obvious beauty had me enchanted for a moment. But, mystical or not, if she didn't want to join us, then maybe she was on the wrong side.

Did she see me as a Jew? Did she see me as an enemy?
Someone she wanted evicted, arrested, or dead?

What I imagined her thinking fueled me forward, shoulder to shoulder with the protesting crowd. From the synagogue, the mass of citizens continued toward Sveta Nedelya at a slower pace. But all I cared about was finally being in the middle of the action. In this moment, I was literally in the center of a wave of concerned Bulgarians—men and women, young and old—pushing ahead, urging the nation toward progress. Justice.

I found myself behind an elderly man in priestly robes, moving slowly.

"Rabbi Zion!" I shouted.

"Misho!"

He looked just as shocked to see me. But instead of giving me a fatherly scolding or grabbing my hand and leading me back to Stefan's car, he cracked a smile.

"You taught me something the other day, son," he

confessed above the rumbling of the crowd. "To not be afraid."

"But I didn't say that."

"You didn't have to," he yelled back. "Sometimes God's message gets to us indirectly."

I smiled and he grabbed my hand and said, "God be with you, Misho."

I thanked him with a nod. In the ebb and flow of the massive crowd, I was soon separated from the rabbi.

Now my body was bursting with energy—tingly from head to toe.

Why?

I was finally free—out in the world again and expressing myself along with thousands of others. Me, my family, the rabbi, my *people* deserved the rights of citizens—the rights that had been stripped by the Nazi regime. Our time had come. Our voices were being heard. And I was part of this wave that demanded justice and protection from the government.

That's how I felt in those moments leading up to the clash with the military police.

In retrospect, I suppose what came next was inevitable. *What fascist government allows its citizens to speak out openly against it?*

As we neared the church at the end of Maria Luisa Boulevard, the police blockade ahead of our group came into plain sight. Soon the bodies around me were packed in tighter, some grumbling, others shouting obscenities at the police. One voice rang out above the others: "Save our Jewish neighbors!" Others began to repeat the slogan, but that was quickly interrupted by a few screams where the frontline protesters met the batons and bayonets of the military police. With the crowd moving every which way, I could barely keep my feet without falling down.

Helpless, with chaos on all sides, I braced myself, knowing that if I did fall I'd probably be trampled to death. But I pushed forward; I hadn't joined the march just to run away at the first sign of a challenge. The crowd quickly thinned out, and chaos took over. I turned around to see formerly courageous protesters fleeing like scared hens. The next thing I knew, someone pushed me from the side, and my hands and knees hit the gravelly ground. Though it hurt, I scrambled to get up as fast as I could.

Almost instantly, a hand grabbed me near the armpit to help pull me up.

The face was familiar.

It was the teenage boy who had rallied the crowd back at Nevski Cathedral.

With his support, I stood up. As I brushed the gravel off my hands, a blunt object struck me in the back of the head.

That's the last thing I remembered of the march.

PETER

It wasn't the fact that I was locked in a jail cell that depressed me.

It was the sense of defeat—the knowledge that the people's call for justice and a better government had been crushed so quickly. So easily. It hurt to be so full of hope and then brutally deflated all within the span of twenty minutes.

The narrow jail cell reeked of urine, vomit, and cheap chemical cleaning fluid all wrapped in one. My head throbbed and my shoulders and ribs ached from the beating I'd taken at the hands of uniformed officers of the state.

Worst of all, I'd been given endless hours to just sit and reflect . . .

On the danger David still faced—the threat of his family being evicted or killed.

On the decision to go to Sofia and appeal to Parliament member Peshev.

On the moment I upset my dad when I told him I'd stay in Sofia and fight.

On the pretty young woman who had come to Ioan's apartment with the inside information.

What was it all for, if the Jews were still being evicted?

I thought about the failed attempt to kill Belev, of Ioan being shot and collapsing down onto the cobblestones, lifeless. *Was sacrificing his life all for nothing?*

I pondered the lost opportunity for the Bulgarian people to unite and fight against the pro-Nazi police ruling the street that day. *Would I stay in prison? Would they execute me for treason?*

As defeated and alone as I felt, I wasn't actually alone.

The boy, who was around my age, was laid out on the bench against the wall. I had tried to help him up as the authorities rained down on us with their batons and boots. But he was hit pretty badly, and I was walloped soon after. They arrested dozens of marchers and just happened to throw the two of us into the same cell. What were the chances? This skinny, dark-haired guy, who kind of reminded me of David, had been dazed and mostly unconscious for hours.

Now he moved, touched the back of his head, and groaned. "What the hell?" he said, looking around at the cell. "Are we in jail?"

"Bingo," I said.

He looked at me as if trying to figure out if he knew me or not.

"You're the guy who spoke after Metropolitan Stefan," he said. Then he winced, holding his wounded head. "I followed you and the protestors. Thanks for the help."

"Well, I tried," I said. "Not much help. I'm Peter."

"Um, I'm Misho," he said after hesitating a bit.

"You sure about that?"

He looked around furtively. "My name's Michael. I've been going by Misho ever since the new laws were passed."

"You're Jewish?"

"Yeah."

"Jesus Christ, if they knew . . ." I looked beyond the cell bars and lowered my voice to a whisper. "You'd be sent off to a camp tonight!"

"I just wanted to get into the action," he said.

"Yeah, that's what I thought months ago when I decided to stay in Sofia and join the Front," I told him. "I wanted to be part of the action. You know, be a hero. Feel the glory of war."

As the words left my mouth, they sounded so stupid it pained me.

"And . . . ?" Misho asked.

"I was clueless," I said. "There's nothing heroic about hiding in an apartment."

"Tell me about it," Misho said. "I've been in hiding since January. But at least you're fighting with the Fatherland Front."

I laughed. "What, so I can ramble on about Marx and try to sneak around and kill bad guys every few months? No thanks."

There was a long pause before he spoke. "So why did you rally people to march today?"

"Honestly, I just wanted to do something—anything—to help my friend, David. My neighbors—his family—they're Jewish. The police and the government won't protect them, so someone has to try."

Misho, sitting there with his elbows on his knees, stared into his hands as if they were telling him something important.

"You're right, someone has to try," he said.

"Well, we tried and here we are in jail."

"Is this how it ends?" he asked.

I didn't answer him. *Is this how it ends? Sitting in a jail cell? Awaiting execution?*

Two prison guards opened our cell abruptly.

"*Haide!*" one yelled, and they each grabbed one of Misho's arms and dragged him out. They didn't even look in my direction.

Do they already know he's Jewish?
Are they going to kill him?
Will I be next?

MISHO

My time in the jail cell came to a sudden end when two

guards entered, grabbed me, and dragged me out without a word of warning or explanation. They led me to a stark room where a chiseled man in a dark suit sat at a small table.

One of the guards clamped my hands behind my back with handcuffs, and they closed the door behind them. Then it was just me and the mysterious, sharp-eyed man in a windowless room.

He commanded me to sit, and I did. His sinister voice scared me.

"What's your name?" he demanded.

"Misho."

"Last name?"

I hesitated. "Stefanov."

"Hmm, you paused there," he said. "My last name is Belev—I didn't have to think about it." He stared at me for a few long moments. "Where do you live?"

"In Plovdiv normally," I said. "I'm here with my uncle."

"What's the address?"

"Uh, up near Boulevard Tsankov," I said. "I don't know exactly. I mean, I can get there, I just don't know the street number."

"Don't know your address, huh?" he said, stroking his pointy chin. "Are you a Jew?"

"No, why do you ask?" I said.

"I don't know," Belev said. "Something about your eyes. I have a knack for spotting vermin. It's my job."

At that moment, everything in my chest sunk and shriveled. I felt helpless—as if this anonymous man could take my life by simply snapping his fingers. The metal handcuffs suddenly became icy cold, and the palms of my hands went clammy.

"Does this kind of talk offend you?" he added.

"No, why would it?" I shivered.

"Of course," he said and laughed to himself. "How old are you?"

"Eighteen."

"Just a kid," he said. "And the boy in the cell with you?"

"I don't know."

"You don't know him?"

"No," I said.

"You wouldn't know if he was in the Fatherland Front, for instance?"

"No, sir."

"You're not being very helpful, you know," the man said.

"I'm sorry."

"Do you know what we do to people who are not helpful, Misho?"

"N-no."

Fear welled inside me. My arms and legs grew numb. On the verge of breaking down, I tried desperately to compose myself a little longer.

"We get rid of them," he said. "Because if they are unhelpful, or the opposite of helpful, then they might logically be considered *harmful*. Anyone harmful to the government, to the war effort, is considered dangerous . . . in other words, an enemy. Do you understand me, Misho?"

"Yes."

"Are you Jewish?"

"No."

"Why don't I believe you?" Belev said. "Do you know any Jews in hiding?"

"No, sir."

I lowered my head in shame. I couldn't stop the tears. Two wet lines ran down my cheeks.

"Why are you crying?" he asked, as if he were an alien being who knew nothing of human emotions.

"I'm scared," I said, knowing I was finished. Broken. Done.

"Why are you scared if you have *nothing to hide*?" Belev slammed his fist on the table as he yelled the last few words.

This startled me so badly that my body jumped and my head popped up involuntarily to face him head on. His eyes bulged and watered with rage and hatred. The man had a problem, but it wasn't specifically with me. He didn't know me at all.

As I stared at his boiling face, my fear turned into something else. This man, Belev, was prepared to kill me because his hatred had taken from him everything good in life, and now all he had was the power to kill those whom he saw as enemies. Hatred had consumed him, but the real enemy was inside him, somewhere deep behind the mask he wore.

Strange that this all came to mind as we sat there in a kind of surreal staring match. God only knows what was going through his head. Though my fear had somewhat dissipated, or at least shifted gears, I sensed that my life would end very soon.

A knock on the door interrupted our silent stalemate, and I was beyond shocked to see a large man in black robes enter the room. Archbishop Stefan was accompanied by two police officers, who calmly walked over and uncuffed me.

"You're coming with me, Misho," Stefan said.

Belev stood up and faced Stefan—who looked so big next to the little fascist, it appeared he could eat him for breakfast.

"What the *hell* are you doing?" Belev snapped at Stefan.

"Hell?" Stefan responded coolly. "No need to speak of it now, you'll have plenty of that in your future."

"How dare you!" Belev said and looked at the two police officers in disbelief. "A priest can't interfere in matters . . ."

"Archbishop," Stefan corrected. He handed him a note, which Belev read immediately.

"This is corruption," Belev said, almost gasping in disbelief. "This boy is not a seminary student, he's an enemy of the state. How dare you use your sanctified connections to get around the law!"

"Live by the sword, die by the sword," Stefan replied. "Matthew, Chapter Twenty-Six." He patted me on the back. "Come on, Misho. I'll take you home."

I expected Belev to pull out a gun, or somehow try to prevent the archbishop from escorting me out, but he just stood there with that crazed, eye-bulging look, like he was about to implode.

Stefan walked me down the stark hallway, and I didn't look back. As the archbishop and I exited the building, I pictured Peter in that cold, smelly jail cell and considered making a plea for his case, but we were already outside and I had inconvenienced Stefan more than enough that day.

We hadn't spoken since leaving the interrogation room, but when he handed me the keys to the car, I finally broke the silence.

"Thank you, Archbishop," I said, my tears welling up again and spilling over, despite my attempt to stop them. "I should never have left you like that."

"You did what your heart told you to do, which is no grave sin," he said. "But you also got lucky, kid."

I opened the door and he climbed into the backseat.

"How did you get me out?" I asked.

Stefan sighed and made the sign of the cross.

"It's good to have connections," he said. "And a fair amount of good fortune. Rabbi Daniel Zion was not so fortunate. He's been arrested as well, and they refuse to release him."

My God. I had completely forgotten about the rabbi. One minute he was right by my side, and the next . . . *Had they beaten him up? Would he remain in jail? Would he be deported or executed by the fascists?*

"Will he be okay?" I asked.

Stefan didn't answer.

I got in and drove.

LILY

There was no easy way to tell Belev the news that evening.

He'd been out of the office all day, and now I dreaded the moment he'd appear because I would have to hand him the letter.

It was unsealed, sent around noon from Prime Minister Filov's office.

I ignored the letter for hours, but as time dragged on and Belev hadn't shown his face in the office, I finally took the liberty of reading it.

Dear Belev:

Though the evictions were carried out today as planned (despite the damned demonstrations downtown this morning), a new issue has emerged. It seems that King Boris has intervened and re-directed the trains of Jews marked for deportation via the Danube. New labor camps have been set up within our Bulgarian borders to house the Jews and put them to work HERE. The king insisted that national work projects are necessary for the domestic war effort, so the trains were re-routed. The Nazi regional commander is aware, as well as Herr Hitler himself. I understand that this will disappoint you and KEV's efforts to deport all Jews to Poland as originally planned, but there is no way around it for now. Stand by for further information.

Sincerely,
Prime Minister Filov

Shaking from nerves, I folded the letter neatly, put it back into the envelope, and left it on his desk. It was only a matter of time before Belev walked into the office and read it.

News had spread that many anti-eviction demonstrators had been arrested and others dispersed in the center of downtown. Most likely, Belev was involved in the crackdown orders. It made me wonder about Peter, and that odd, skinny boy with the desperate look on his face. It was crazy to think that a strange boy had wanted me to join the marchers, and even crazier that, for a split second, I had actually thought about it.

Belev entered the office as I was preparing to leave. I greeted him anxiously and told him about the letter on his desk. He passed by me with only a quick glance, went into his office, and picked up the envelope. I expected all hell to break loose—a chilling wail, a burst of profanity, maybe even a chair crashing through the glass window separating his office from our communal work space. But there was no audible reaction. Perhaps he'd already seen enough that day; the news must not have registered that his plan to deport the Jews had failed yet again.

When I peeked through his doorway, his face appeared glazed over, stunned.

"Is everything okay?"

"No," he snapped.

"Can I do anything?"

He looked up at me as if he were surprised at my offer. "You can't change policy, so I suppose you can't do much, Lily."

"The policy is changed?" I played dumb.

"Unfortunately. Domestic labor camps? I don't know what the hell that even means."

I shook my head, showing that I didn't, either.

"The idea that we need Jews to work on national projects is absolutely preposterous!"

"I wouldn't know," I said, assuming Belev would appreciate a docile woman with no strong opinion or understanding of the matter. But he didn't take it that way.

"Wouldn't know what?" he asked.

"Me? Oh, I only meant that I don't know anything about the camps you mentioned."

"Of course you don't, you're just a secretary," he belittled. "But you do know *something* . . ."

He dangled the last two syllables long enough to break my nerves.

Why is he questioning me like this? What does he think I know?

I clenched my hands behind my back in an effort to calm myself down, but my sweaty palms only reinforced my internal hysteria.

"I only know what crosses my desk," I said.

"At Skopje, you were there at the train station with me. You were shaken up."

"Not really," I said, trying to keep my voice steady and stern, hiding any sympathy I had for the thousands who suffered that day.

"It's okay, Lily," he said. "It's natural for a young woman like yourself to get shaken up by a scene like that. But it's not proper for a KEV employee to sympathize with the enemy."

"I agree completely," I said.

"You wouldn't know who's been leaking information from this office, would you, Lily?"

"No, sir," I said with such conviction that I believed it myself. "But I do hope the imposter is found soon."

"Goddamn it!" Belev yelled out suddenly, his frustration finally exploding as he slammed his fist on his desk, making his stack of loose papers jump.

My chest jumped, too.

Belev winced and grabbed the space between his neck and shoulder.

"Are you okay?" I asked, still shaky.

"It's just the stress." He winced again.

"It is very stressful these days," I said as I approached him.

Call it survival instinct.

When my hand landed gently on his shoulder and began to massage lightly, it was an out-of-body experience, almost as if I had no control over my own limbs. A gut reaction. I didn't think about it at all.

"That feels good," he said.

I continued for a minute or two. The only sound that occasionally broke the awkward silence was Belev groaning when my thumb hit the right spot near his shoulder blade.

As abruptly as I'd started, without thinking, I stopped.

Belev turned to me. "Can I take you out for a drink, Lily?"

He is my boss. He has all the power.

He could turn against me at any provocation, and there was enough treason on my hands to justify my swift execution.

"A drink?" I said. "Yes, that sounds nice."

It was my safest option.

$$\underline{\text{III}}$$

SEPT 7, 1944

MISHO

Exactly one year ago—back on September 7, 1943—I had a conversation with Archbishop Stefan about King Boris's mysterious death. I'd jotted our words down in my journal and noted the date.

"So he died of heart failure?" I asked.

"Officially, yes, but . . ."

"But what?"

"They suspect he was poisoned," Stefan said. "The king had just visited Adolf Hitler at his head-quarters. Boris was adamant that no Bulgarian troops be used on the eastern front against Russia, and he must have insisted, again, that Bulgarian Jews stay in Bulgarian labor camps and not be deported."

"Must have?" I asked.

"I don't know the details, I just know Boris," Stefan said. "He may have cooperated with the Nazis and fascists, but he didn't want blood on his hands."

"So Hitler killed him?"

"King Boris did not have a heart problem, Misho," he explained. "Nor was it in his family history, until last week."

"When did he meet with Hitler?

He sighed. "Last week."

That conversation, one year ago, was one of my most memorable talks with Archbishop Stefan. Not only because he sullenly explained to me the mysterious death of King Boris—perhaps the main source of Jewish protection throughout the war—but because it came at a time when the Bulgarian government was shifting. The right-wing fascists who had pushed for Jewish deportation were moving out, and a more moderate pro-Nazi government had entered the fray. The anti-Jewish measures remained in place, but the push for eviction and deportation had slowed. Maybe this was because in the fall of 1943, the Allies began bombing Sofia, and the war had clearly swung in the Allies' favor.

Now, a year later, I spoke to Stefan again, but our conversation was memorable for a different reason. The Russians had beaten back the Nazis and were pushing into Eastern Europe with a string of victories. The Soviet Army, Stefan told me, would be entering Bulgaria very soon. The British and the Americans had been dropping bombs on Sofia over the past year without much resistance. Threats of Jewish deportation to concentration camps in Poland had all but disappeared. There were still domestic labor camps for Jews, but the men were actually working on roads and other public works, with no reports of poor treatment or any threat of death. Nonetheless, me, my mother and sister, and many others remained in hiding as long as the Nazi threat existed. *Who knew if things would swing back into Hitler's favor?*

That is, until Stefan spoke. "Misho, they haven't publicized it yet, but the German officials and soldiers have left Sofia."

"What? Seriously?" I asked with a huge smile on my

face.

"Yes, and their Bulgarian collaborators are hanging on by a string."

"What do you mean?"

"Our national government and the fascists who control it could be pushed out of power any day now," Stefan said.

"And what does that mean for me?" I asked.

"It means you'll be free soon."

It didn't seem real—the idea of having a real life after hiding for so long.

LILY

Over a year has gone by without writing down a word about my life.

I must confess that my silence was due to my own shame.

But, please, reader, understand that I only did it under the extraordinary conditions of war. I did it as an instinctual response. I did it for my survival.

I had an affair with Alexander Belev—or Alex, as I began to call him.

Yesterday, September 7, 1944, I met Alex at a small restaurant in Lozenets.

I hadn't seen him for weeks. Our office had closed a month earlier, and the only work we underlings had in those final days was to destroy the incriminating documents that filled our filing cabinets. The KEV department, the source of our paychecks, no longer legally existed.

Alex—Belev—telephoned me to meet him at a restaurant. We hadn't spoken to each other for a while. I figured he would make the termination of both my employment and our relationship official, but maybe he would help me find a new job somewhere else. *Why else would he want to meet me at the final hour?* Everyone I knew accepted it as fact: the Russians were coming and the war would be ending soon.

So I expected no more than a formal layoff and a goodbye from Alexander Belev that evening. Our relationship had ignited, sparked into flame, and slowly extinguished over the course of that year. My intense fear of him had dissipated as he showed me his softer side. And then, when I suppose he'd satisfied his curiosities, Alex became distant and cold, treating me like a dumb girl again. His awkward greetings in the office became normal, and then he stopped asking me out altogether. He became "Belev" again.

I went along with it all. I suppose I could have been offended at the thought of him using me to fulfill his sexual desires, but I never forgot one thing—*I was using him, too.*

Like I said, I did what was necessary in order to survive. Still, I couldn't shake the sense of shame that filled me when I sat down across from him at the restaurant that evening.

"Did you walk here alone, Lily?" he asked.

"Yes," I said.

It was the first time I heard fear quiver so clearly in his voice. He peered out the window as if he expected a gang of armed men to be waiting for him on the sidewalk.

"I have to leave."

"I figured as much," I said.

"When the Soviets arrive, there's no telling what they'll do to me. To us."

"To us?"

"Working at the KEV is no small thing, Lily," he said. "To them, we're the enemy. Do you understand what conquering armies do to their enemies? Russians, no less?"

"I hadn't thought about it that way," I admitted.

He didn't know I'd helped the opposing side during the war. *I was the leak—the spy.* Surely, that would exonerate me from the list of enemies, though I would never share this tidbit with Belev.

"Lily, I don't know what they'll do to you, but they will certainly arrest me. Perhaps worse."

"Worse?" I asked uneasily. "Execution?"

"It's very possible," Belev said. "There's often swift retribution in these cases."

His eyes watered with pure self-concern. I didn't know what to say.

"Lily, I am leaving Sofia. I have an escape plan that nobody else in the world knows about. I'll be crossing the border at Kyustendil into Macedonia. I have a fake passport and a connection in Skopje. From there I will go to Germany—I have many connections there. The war is far from over, but getting out of Bulgaria is a must."

"Well, that's quite a plan," I said.

I couldn't help but see him as a pathetic coward. A man who had planned the deaths of tens of thousands was now going to great lengths to save himself from the consequences of the job he was once so proud of.

"I want you to come with me, Lily."

The offer was so unexpected, I almost laughed. Instead, I bit my lip and stayed silent.

"I can help you get a job in Germany. Or we can move to Spain, maybe even South America. Think about the adventure."

Unable to look him in the eye, I gazed down at my glass of water and thought to myself: *This man was my boss. This man was my lover. This man is disgusting. I want to tell him what I did, right now—that I sabotaged his entire Nazi-inspired purpose and his planning and management of the whole dreadful operation.* I wanted to tell him right then and there, but fear still had its grip on me.

I looked Belev in the eye before speaking. "No, thank you," I said. "I can't leave my parents behind."

His gaze dropped to the salt and pepper holders.

"Are you sure?" he asked. "It will be dangerous for you here."

"I'm sure," I said without hesitation, ashamed that I didn't have the courage to say more.

"I was afraid you'd say that." With that, Belev appeared as though he might reach across the table and slap me. Instead, he reached below the table and pulled out a bound filing box I hadn't noticed before.

"These are official papers—some documents I will use to write my memoirs," he said. "Remember how I told you it's my dream to write a book one day?"

"Yes," I said, flashing back to the time we were lying in bed and he had momentarily opened up to me, telling me all his self-consumed plans to write about himself.

"Well, I can't risk taking them across borders," he said. "Besides, they'll weigh me down. I'd like you to put them somewhere safe for me, and I will send for them to be shipped later."

I had to bite my tongue to keep myself from shouting, "Go to hell! Keep your goddamned documents! Nobody will read your stupid book, anyway!"

Before I could muster the confidence to speak, Belev stood up, muttered a weak goodbye, turned his back, and was gone.

PETER

Max was the only guy from the Fatherland Front that I'd become friends with.

We stood on the balcony and smoked cigarettes that night.

He listened as I lamented what my existence had become.

That year, after being released from three months of imprisonment, I'd fallen into the same daily routine. I would get up and make myself coffee and toast, then wait for a Fatherland Front messenger to give me news of some action to be taken. The action was never soldier-like. It would often consist of running food or news to comrades in hiding, or to connected families in need. After the Americans started dropping bombs on the city, the need to help victims sort through the rubble, and to lend a hand in other ways, increased. But aside from that, I was simply surviving—hiding in Ioan's apartment alone, feeling guilty that I blew the one big opportunity I had the year before: to kill the man directly responsible for the attempted deportation and death of Jews, including Ioan's death. *Alexander Belev.*

Max sighed and took a big drag of his cigarette. He had heard it all before.

"Are you finished?" he said.

"Yeah."

"You're looking at the negative side of the situation, Comrade. Think about what's happening now," Max exclaimed. "The fascists are gone! They've been run out of town, out of the whole country, and guess who's taking over now?"

"The Soviet Army?" I guessed.

"No, but they will help us," he said confidently. "They're our communist comrades, Peter! The brilliant thing is that now we will be in charge."

"We?"

"Yes, we, the Fatherland Front. All of your weeks and months of boring service to the cause is going to pay off! You'll see, the last meeting made it very clear. The Germans and their fascist followers have fled. The current government is full of traitors and weak apologists who will soon be removed. The Fatherland Front will be taking over soon."

"When?"

"Tomorrow, the next day—hell, I don't know!" Max said excitedly. "But we are the only ones who have a record of resisting the enemy, supporting the people, and protecting the capital."

"This city is in ruins," I said. "Have you looked outside lately?"

"You don't get it, do you? Now *we* will control the government, and guys like *us* will get rewarded. Think about the opportunities! We will be given favored positions in Sofia's government. I already have some connections. Who knows, I might become the chief of police one day; you might become a Parliament member or the next Minister of Defense!"

He inhaled a ton of smoke and then quickly exhaled.

"What, you've got nothing to say, Peter?"

"I think I'm done," I said.

"What?"

"I'm going back to Kyustendil."

"You're kidding, right? Turning your back on all this opportunity?"

"I didn't join the Front for opportunity," I clarified. "I wanted to protect my friend and his family—to fight against Nazis. And now I'm living in a dead man's apartment, the Nazis are gone, and my friend and my family are back in Kyustendil. So I'm gonna go."

Dumbfounded, Max stared at me, his mouth agape.

"Peter, you'll regret that."

"Maybe, but I can only do what feels right. And that means going home."

Max shook his head slowly, finished his cigarette, and wished me luck. We walked to the front entrance together. Before he made it out the door, I had to say it.

"Max, one last thing."

"Yeah?"

"When you find yourself in a position of power, don't forget, okay?"

"Forget what?"

"What it was like to be us," I said. "To be the underdogs. To be the victims of a corrupted government."

"I won't," he said easily.

"Because they say it's easy to forget, you know, once you're the one in power."

Max stared at me as if I'd just given him complicated directions to an unknown neighborhood.

"Just do the right thing for me," I said and smiled at him.

"Okay," he said, looking serious. "I will."

We shook hands, and Max closed the door behind him.

I went to pack my things.

SEPT 8, 1944

MISHO

As I sat at the wooden seminary table alone, over a bowl of bland oatmeal, images of the previous night's dreams came back to me.

The woman in the red coat I'd spoken to right after Peter's rallying speech—she was in my dream. I grabbed her hand and told her to join the protest again. She walked with me for a minute but was clearly scared. We were surrounded by the mob. She let go of my hand and said, "I did something good, I promise. But I can't join you." I tried to grab her hand, but she just repeated, "I did something good," and slipped into the crowd, out of sight. It didn't make any sense to me.

The boy, Peter—the one I had followed in the march and spoken to briefly in that prison cell—he was in my dream, too. We were back in the jail cell, except he was the one who'd been beaten up badly and I was perfectly fine. Not a scratch.

I said, "I'm gonna get you out of here."

He said, "No, save yourself."

I replied, "I'm sick of saving myself. I've been hiding too long. I need to do something real."

"Real?" he asked. "What does that even mean?"

Peter repeated, "Save yourself!" as the guards burst in and pulled me out the door.

My oatmeal was getting cold. I dug through it and tried to make sense of both visitors in my subconscious.

Why did she say, "I did something good, I promise"?

What did she do, and why did I care? Was that what the war was all about—did you do the right thing? Did you act on the right side of history or just save yourself while others suffered and died? Had I been selfish by hiding? Had I done the wrong thing all along?

Stefan snapped me out of my thoughts by plopping down at the opposite side of the table. He laid out a newspaper next to his bowl.

"Good news today, Misho," he said. "Remarkable, actually."

"What—the war is over?"

"Almost, for Bulgaria at least," he replied. "They say the prime minister and Parliament repealed the anti-Jewish laws and have closed the labor camps. Jewish people will be returning to their homes soon. You will no longer need to hide or live in fear."

"How can we be sure?" I asked. "What if the government just changes their minds?"

"Well, it wasn't God who touched their hearts. The politicians realized that if they don't repeal and erase all these Nazi measures, then the Soviet army and the Allies will treat them as the enemy. And, who knows, they could all be put in prison."

"They're doing this now so they *don't* seem like Nazi collaborators? To save themselves?"

"Exactly."

"Well, I hope they get caught," I said.

"Be careful what you wish for, Misho," the archbishop said. "It might be worse than jail. They might be executed. Either before or after the Red Army arrives."

"When will the Russians arrive?" I asked.

"Soon," he said.

"Today? Tomorrow?"

"I know what you're really asking, Misho," Stefan said and crossed his arms. "You will be free to go and should prepare to leave soon. Everything is changing these days, thank God."

Then I remembered the rabbi.

"And what about Rabbi Zion?" I added. "Will he be released from prison?"

"Yes . . . if he's still alive."

LILY

All morning, I drank ersatz coffee and contemplated my options—staying in Sofia, or going home. I would be safer in Stara Zagora, but there would be no jobs, no future. *I can visit my parents, but then what? Return to Sofia when the smoke clears?*

Belev would be sneaking out of the city, using dirt roads to avoid checkpoints, maybe even traveling in disguise. The thought of being on the train next to him sent shivers up my neck. I couldn't believe I'd had a romantic relationship with that man just to save myself. Now it was over, and all I felt was shame. Guilt. Regret. I pictured Belev crossing the border into Macedonia and meeting up with his Nazi contacts who would get him a flight to Berlin. I pictured his arrogant expression as he sat at a cafe on the Unter den Linden with fellow Nazis. They would salute him for successfully sending 10,000 Macedonian and Greek Jews to their deaths. He would be praised. Promoted. *And then he would contact me to send off his precious box of KEV documents?* I couldn't stand the thought of it.

I'd left Belev's box of papers next to the coat hanger in the entryway. I paced over to the box and kicked it, resolving to do one last thing in the name of decency and my own conscience.

I grabbed a pen and notepad and left my apartment abruptly.

When I hit Rakovski Street, signs of change in the city were already clear. Raggedy uniformed soldiers of the Fatherland Front were parading through the street. These unorganized communists held rifles and banners that said "Fascist Scum Are Gone" and "Socialism and Freedom for Bulgaria" and "Working Class United." It put me on edge because, only weeks before, the Fatherland Front had been termed a terrorist group. Now they seemed to be taking over the city, maybe the national government. If Belev was right, these makeshift partisan soldiers parading down the middle of the street could stop me, question me, find out about my previous employer, and arrest me. At that moment I decided: after this last self-appointed mission, I would gather my things and take the next train to Stara Zagora.

I continued walking down Rakovski past Dundukov Street. As I turned left at the church and onto Tsar Simeon Street, my simple scheme solidified in my head. I would knock on Ioan Goodman's door and speak to him or the boy, Peter, about my final offering of valuable confidential information: the escape plan of former KEV director Alexander Belev. If they could stop him before he crossed the border, then justice could be served. If nobody was home, then I would leave a note with the information, slide it under the door, and leave—my final attempt to make up for my wrongs.

A crippling fear shot through my veins as I stepped up the creaky stairs at Tsar Simeon 78. It was impossible to know if returning to the flat was putting myself in greater danger. What if the Fatherland Front was narrowly focused on retribution and wanted people like me arrested or killed? There was no way of knowing, but I figured I could play the ignorant female messenger. Then I recalled the old saying: don't shoot the messenger.

Please don't.

My hand shaking, I knocked on Ioan Goodman's door—first lightly and then progressively harder. I banged loudly until my knuckles stung. Nobody was home or willing to answer. I pulled out my notepad and leaned on the door. I wrote:

Message to the Fatherland Front. Former KEV director Alexander Belev is trying to escape into Macedonia through the border at Kyustendil today. He is guilty of murdering 11,343 Jews.

Sincerely,
The Spy

I signed it this way because I would never sign my real name; besides, if the boy, Peter, read it, he would know it was from me and that I could be trusted.

Thinking I heard a noise inside, I knocked hard one last time, then folded the note and shoved it under the door.

PETER

In the middle of packing my duffle bag, I heard someone knocking on the front door.

It would be just my luck to be shot on my last day in Sofia before leaving for home. Though I was aware that the Fatherland Front was parading through the streets and would soon take over the government, I also expected some final skirmishes—last attempts by nasty fascists to hold onto power, or at least go down fighting.

Which was why, as soon as I heard loud knocking at the door, I grabbed Ioan's loaded rifle from the closet. I scurried quietly behind the couch, positioned myself on one knee, and placed the barrel of the gun on the cushion. My weapon was pointed square in the middle of that front door. There was a pause in the knocking and I could hear the door squeaking from the weight of someone leaning on it. *Are they going to try and break the door down? Is it one, two, three people out there? Are they police? Armed? Friends or enemies?*

There was no way to tell who it was, and if I yelled to ask their identity it could turn out to be my last words. So I held my aim, unlatched the safety, and placed my finger lightly on the trigger. *Wouldn't it be ironic if I were to kill someone—or be killed—on the last day of my service to the partisan cause, when my comrades were already parading around and celebrating their victory in the streets?*

I waited at the ready, careful to not accidentally apply too much pressure on the trigger. Loud knocking came again and I twitched, almost pulling the trigger from nerves and fright. Whoever was on the other side of that door was millimeters from death.

When I heard the sound of footsteps going off down the hall, I took my finger off the trigger and approached the door, only to see a small note on the floor.

I whispered the words out loud, as if there were a comrade standing next to me: "Alexander Belev is trying to escape into Macedonia through the border at Kyustendil today. He is guilty of murdering 11,343 Jews. Sincerely . . ."

The Spy?

I ran to the balcony and looked directly down at the sidewalk four floors below me. A blonde woman exited the building, and though I couldn't see her face, it had to be her—the attractive girl who'd visited once before and leaked information about the deportation of Jews. *The Spy.* I didn't even know her name.

I picked up the phone to call home, but the line was dead. I'd forgotten it had been months since the telephones in Ioan's apartment worked. I had to get the news to Kyustendil. We had to capture Belev before he crossed the border. Within minutes, my bag was packed and I was hustling down the stairs. I ran the entire way to the central train station, hopping over piles of bricks and debris from the months of bombings. On the way, I saw a few Fatherland Front comrades policing the streets.

It reminded me of what Max had said about opportunity, and confirmed my decision: I didn't want to be in Sofia anymore.

I could end my own internal war and finally do my part today.

If I found Belev.

MISHO

I stood at my usual smoking spot in the courtyard and remembered Rabbi Zion running toward the car and demanding to go to the May protests on that fateful day. *Is he still alive? Is he in prison? If so, will he be released soon?* Maybe he'd been freed already and I was next. I lit a fresh cigarette as Stefan approached me along a gravel path.

"Put that away, son," he said.

"This?" I asked, pointing to my cigarette. "I've been smoking for over a year now and you've never told me to stop before."

Stefan took the cigarette from my hand and stamped it out on the ground.

"That's because I knew you were dealing with the stress of the war—the loneliness, separation from family—all of it, by smoking. I let it slide because of the circumstances. But that's over. Our war is over, too."

"How can you be so sure?"

"The reports are clear. The Soviet army has entered Bulgaria from Romania. They will be in Sofia in a matter of days. We don't know what to expect exactly, but they're not expected to be aggressive. Perhaps they will help form the new government, or take it over themselves. What I do know is that the anti-Jewish policies are ancient history. You can leave here tonight if you want to, though I suggest you wait until tomorrow morning when there are trains running to Plovdiv."

"Have you heard from my mom?"

"She's in Plovdiv with your sister, at your aunt's house. I will give you their address."

"So just like that, it's over?" I said. "War doesn't make

any sense."

"No, it doesn't," Stefan said. "Which is why I don't want you to worry about it."

"Worry?"

"I know you wanted to leave. You wanted to fight. I almost lost you, but got lucky that day when I found you in jail. If they had discovered you're Jewish, who knows what would have happened."

I didn't like thinking about my short-lived attempt to do something meaningful. Mainly because it was such a failure. It could have been the end for me. But I hated being the victim, or the one that hid out to avoid becoming the victim. I didn't want to tell any of this to Stefan because he'd helped me. He'd saved me. I should have been nothing but grateful for that and for my new freedom, but I was all mixed up.

"You're still conflicted, I can tell," he said.

"How do you know?" I asked, amazed as always at his ability to read me.

"When you get older, you can see these things."

Stefan reached into his pocket and pulled out some *leva* bills.

"Here you go, Misho. For the train ticket and food tomorrow."

"Thank you, Archbishop." I said. "For everything."

"I almost forgot, you're not Misho anymore. You're Michael again."

It sounded so strange. Like my war identity was dead and I could now return to my old self. Back to normal. But there was no way to go back to who I was before. I was forever changed by my war experience.

"This is so weird," I said. "I should be overjoyed—but

I don't know what to feel."

"It's because you know that one phase of your life has ended, a new one will begin, and you have no choice in the matter. This particular transition is clear-cut, which is not always the case in life. And when something terrible happens, like this war that continues in Europe and around the world, it's difficult to be optimistic."

"Maybe I'll feel different tomorrow," I said.

"Maybe," Stefan replied. "But my feelings are also mixed. It seems we have won the battle to save thousands of Jewish lives in this nation, but we don't know the damage elsewhere, or what our next battle will be. If the Soviets do take control of this country, then what will it mean for the Church? Josef Stalin is not exactly a pious man. And I am no communist, nor will I ever be converted to that particular ideology—neither for practical reasons or by force. So, we shall see."

"Are you afraid?"

"Never. Not with God by my side."

I didn't know what to say. I didn't believe in God quite like Stefan did.

"You don't have to believe, Misho—I mean, Michael," he corrected himself, miraculously reading my mind again. "You just have to do the right thing. Use this experience to shape your sense of responsibility to others. Be good and spread that goodness. Develop the courage to do the right thing the next time everything around you seems to be going in the wrong direction."

"Thank you," I said again and grinned, recalling the first time I'd met this holy man. "Your Majesty."

Stefan laughed. He remembered, too.

"Now get some rest," he said as he turned and

distanced himself with a few steps. "You'll be traveling tomorrow morning."

He walked away and my eye fell to my trampled cigarette, wasted on the ground. I put my hand in my pocket to grab another, but stopped myself. Stefan was right. I only smoked because I didn't know what else to do. I didn't know how to cope.

Now the war was over.

Almost.

SEPT 9, 1944

LILY

The next train to Stara Zagora was at eleven o'clock that morning.

As usual, I left my apartment early to get *banitsa* and fruit at the nearby market before the meager supply was gone. I wanted to eat well before traveling most of the day.

When I returned to my place fifteen minutes later, the front door was ajar. I thought I might have carelessly left it that way, until I entered and found two skinny, haggard men in makeshift police uniforms inside. They drew their guns at me. Shocked into near paralysis, I made an odd squealing noise and almost fainted. The one with the thick mustache put his pistol back in his holster.

"Are you Lily Dimitrova?" he asked.

"Yes," I said.

"Did you work for the KEV?"

"Yes," I said.

"Miss Dimitrova, we need to put you in handcuffs while we search your apartment."

It wasn't a question or a request. They were now in charge in my own apartment. They moved me over to a chair, and the clean-shaven one with beady eyes bound my hands behind my back with cold steel handcuffs. His clumsy way with them and the untidiness of their uniforms raised my suspicions.

"Are you government agents or city police officers?"

The man with the mustache laughed. "We're with the

Fatherland Front," he said. "And now we *are* the police."

"And you are fascist scum," the other said.

"No. I didn't—"

"Save it, woman, we're not here to interrogate you."

"I'm no fascist," I said. "I actually helped *your* cause."

"We'll see about that," he said, looking incredulous.

I tried to breathe normally and keep my mind from horrible scenarios of post-war chaos and martial law—a world ruled by scruffy partisans who just happened to survive. As my mind began to settle on the idea that I would be exonerated for my work *against* the KEV and the pro-Nazi government—as well as my cooperation with the Fatherland Front men, such as Peter and Ioan—I noticed that the beady-eyed policeman had opened Belev's box and was flipping through it.

"Come see this," he said to his partner.

The mustached one, who seemed the more civilized of the two, scanned a few of Belev's documents, which were sitting there front and center as if they were a gift to these imposters.

"We're going to have to arrest you, Miss Dimitrova," he stated.

"No," I pleaded. "I'm on your side, really."

"That's not what these documents say."

The mustached officer grabbed my arm and led me away.

The other man followed us, cradling Belev's box.

MISHO

Stefan handed me a slip of paper with an address in

Plovdiv. At that moment, I realized that my reunion with my mom and sister was actually going to happen.

The archbishop hugged me and said, "Go."

It was no time to cry or rejoice or give a speech. Our goodbye had been said the night before. I walked outside of the seminary walls and didn't look back. Misho no longer existed. I was Michael again—or some new version of him.

I walked straight down Smirnenski Boulevard, looking around at the dilapidated, bombed-out buildings, weary pedestrians, stray dogs, everything, as if I were seeing it for the first time. Brick rubble and debris littered the streets here and there—the remnants of a year of Allied bombing—seemingly at random throughout the center of the city. As I neared Journalist Square, I almost fell into a four-meter-wide crater that consumed the sidewalk and half the street. Trash filled its bottom half, as if it had become the neighborhood dumpster. I gazed up at the empty sky and sarcastically thanked imaginary B-24 bombers for "liberating" us.

Stepping onto the trolley, a sense of freedom and hope swept over me. The trolley car was almost empty but, miraculously, it was running. As we rolled down the street I observed war-damaged streets and buildings here and there, but people were out walking, shopping for essential items, and cleaning up. An open-air market, though low on supplies, was open. A baba carried her loaf of bread. A young boy kicked a ball against a wall. Life was continuing on.

It was an odd feeling to not be in danger anymore. The authorities were not hunting down Jews. Finally, I had the basic rights of any decent citizen again. And now, at eighteen, I had the freedom of an adult. But along with adulthood came the loss of innocence. If that hadn't been clear to me before leaving Stefan's seminary, it became crystal clear as the trolley turned up Graf Ignatiev and headed closer to the train station.

My trolley car paused at the intersection of Graf Ignatiev and Rakovski. I only recall that moment because it was when I witnessed a woman being escorted down the sidewalk with what appeared to be policemen on both sides of her. As they neared my waiting trolley, I recognized her—it was the blonde woman in the red coat from my dream! It had been over a year since I'd seen her in front of Nevski Cathedral and futilely asked her to join the protest march. I pressed my face to the window to get her attention, but she didn't look anywhere near me. And her expression was one of pure misery and defeat.

Instinct told me to save the girl from those accosting her. But as I bolted to the doors, the trolley began moving forward in the opposite direction of the woman. I stared at her as the distance between us increased. She looked as if she hadn't even dressed for the day, and the men looked rough. They were in a hurry. I continued to stare through the window, wondering what she had done to be arrested right after the war ended, and how that might be connected to why she hadn't joined me in the march. *Maybe she was a Nazi?*

All thoughts of the mysterious young woman disappeared when the trolley veered off of Graf Ignatiev and swung in front of the main city courthouse. The trolley jerked to a stop; too many people were in the middle of the street, blocking it. The driver honked his horn at them. I turned to the opposite window to see the huge bronze lions guarding the Sofia Courthouse, and realized why the crowd was staring in that direction. Below those bronze symbols of justice, a row of loosely organized militia men were lined up with their rifles pointed forward. About five meters in front of them, ten blindfolded men were on their knees close to the courthouse wall. One man stood in front of them, maybe a meter closer to what was obviously a firing squad. The man in front was not blindfolded and in a darker uniform, with a swastika armband. I knew what was going to happen, I just didn't know when. As the trolley lurched forward, I heard two loud pops and watched the Nazi man crumble to the concrete sidewalk. There was a shriek from one of the men on his knees. Another shot rang out, and about a dozen scattered shots followed. Blood splattered against the courthouse wall and the men slumped down, falling backward, forward, and sideways, awkwardly and grotesquely lifeless.

The trolley continued to inch forward, and I gazed at the gruesome scene, suddenly worried about the new change in power. And the Soviet army hadn't even arrived yet!

As if I hadn't seen enough from this single trolley ride, there was more. With the courthouse behind us and every other building now destroyed, we rolled down Maria Luisa Boulevard—near the place where I had marched and then been beaten and jailed. That made me think of Peter, the boy who had tried to help me—the one in the cell with me. *Where is he now? Alive or dead? Back home with his Jewish friend? Or part of an impromptu firing squad—getting back at his jailers?*

We came to a stop in front of the synagogue where we had picked up Rabbi Zion and were shot at by police as we sped off. It made me think about my first and last moments with the rabbi, and gave me faith that he had survived imprisonment. Perhaps what Stefan had told me was true: I had done more than just hide and wait. I had protested in the streets. We had saved a rabbi. *Did this mean I would go straight to shamayim?*

I turned my attention back to the sacred building. The synagogue was almost surrounded by normal citizens—Jews and Gentiles—helping repair the outside walls that had been graffitied and vandalized over the past three years. Part of me wanted to join them, but a larger part ached to see my mother and sister and escape from the chaos of the capital.

As the trolley car eased into the intersection, I spotted the old Islamic mosque across the street. It gave me an odd sort of comfort. It was a reminder that this country had gone through religious persecution before and come out on the other side. Bulgarians had endured and survived that test, and so we would survive and flourish again.

By the time I made it to the train station, partially bombed but still operating, I was emotionally exhausted. I had the next three hours on a train to contemplate it all. Play back all of my moments with Stefan. His eccentric words of wisdom. His sometimes shocking responses. His sage advice. *Did I thank him enough for saving me? Did he know how important his impact was on me? Would I ever see him again?*

When I finally reunited with my mom and sister, a surge of love consumed me. This was why I needed to survive. We spent that whole day together, hugging, smiling, grateful that we had made it through the war alive. We laughed. We prayed. We cried.

They asked very few questions about my experience in hiding, and I read in their expressions that we needn't retell nor, in the process, relive all our bad memories of the war. In fact, there was a certain understood code of silence. I followed suit. Burying the past was almost a necessity.

I only unearthed my wartime experience years later, when I heard about Archbishop Stefan's resignation. Under pressure from the Soviet regime to conform to their doctrines, Stefan refused to cooperate with the communist government. After resigning, he disappeared from public view. He preferred to be exiled to a remote monastery than to compromise his beliefs. It angered me to learn of the regime's mistreatment of the archbishop, but it also made me proud to envision that unique holy man, cursing and defiant till the end. I recalled many of the Biblical quotes he often used, but the one that stuck with me wasn't from Scripture. Maybe because it was the least expected and the shortest.

It might have been a flippant comment by the archbishop, offered up only to calm a young man's foolish desire for wartime adventure, but I don't quite remember it that way. For me, that quote was a foreshadowing sign from a sanctified man. And finally, after I had half-buried my past, it came back to me: "The pen is mightier than the sword."

I needed to dig my story up and write it all down.

LILY

They pushed me into a small, dark cell, locked the door, and left me in there for hours. Who were *they*? The new self-proclaimed police force? The makeshift government?

I cried on the floor of that dark cell. I should've been on a train to see my parents. Belev's box of incriminating papers should *not* have been in my possession!

When two different men entered, picked me up, and escorted me down the hallway, they were no kinder or gentler than the first two provisional cops who had ruined my day.

They put me in a larger room with no windows and a single chair, which they handcuffed me to, hands behind my back, and abruptly left. Normally I would have said something—asked what they were doing, demanded my rights—but I was too disoriented. Alone in that room, I tried to gather myself. I was not supposed to be here. I was innocent, and whoever came in to speak with me would understand that fact by the end of whatever the hell this was, and I would leave Sofia and the whole war behind me.

A stocky man with a dark mustache and short hair entered the room. He appeared to be in his thirties, but when he opened his mouth his half-rotten teeth aged him by at least ten years.

"Who are you?" I asked. "Why am I here?"

"The officers who arrested you were surprised," he said.

"Am I supposed to ask why?"

"They didn't expect a young, attractive woman like you." He adjusted himself.

"Well, surprise," I said.

"You don't seem to think this is serious, Miss Dimitrova."

"I don't even know what *this* is," I stated. "I am innocent, yet I'm bound to this chair, in this room, speaking to . . . who are you?"

My attitude was sharp, because everything about my arrest was unjust.

The man leaned against the wall in front of me and ogled me creepily for a long moment.

"Who I am is not your concern right now," he said.

"Do you work for the government?" I asked.

"The government is in a process of transition right now," he said rather confidently. "I work for the police force under the transition government."

"Transitioning until the Soviets arrive?"

"They are our comrades, Miss Dimitrova, so you need not worry. Are you a comrade?"

"Am I a communist? No."

"Are you or were you a Nazi?"

"No," I stated.

"Didn't you work for the KEV?"

"Yes, I did, but—"

"A distinctly fascist, pro-Nazi branch of government, Miss Dimitrova, so how does that not make you a Nazi sympathizer and, by direct association, an employee of Adolf Hitler?"

"You don't understand, I—"

"Was Alexander Belev your boss?"

"Yes," I admitted. There was no point in denying it. "But I—"

"Do you know he is a card-carrying member of the

Nazi party and is responsible for the deaths of thousands of Jews in greater Bulgaria?"

"Well, yes," I said. "But he was my *boss*. I didn't—"

"Do you know where he is right now?"

"Let me speak!" I yelled, halfway out of my mind from all the interruptions. "I did work for the KEV, and Belev, but I *also* worked for the other side. I leaked information to a Jewish doctor and then to members of the Fatherland Front in order to *stop* the deportation of Jews."

The crude man appeared taken aback. He put his hands in his pockets, as if he were civilized.

"Who was this Jewish doctor?" he asked with a hint of curiosity.

"Dr. Levi," I said. "He was evicted and sent to a labor camp. I think."

"His first name?"

I drew in my breath. "I don't know," I said. "His office is on Budapeshta Street. I don't know the address number, but I could find it for you. When he left—was evicted—last year, they closed the office."

"I see, Miss . . . a doctor with no first name and no office address," he remarked snidely. "And who were the Fatherland Front members you worked with?"

"Ioan . . . um, Goodman," I said. "And Peter something. I don't know his last name."

The man stood there nodding his head, then shaking it. His hands remained in his pockets.

"Aren't you going to write down these names and check?" I asked. "I'm quite certain they will vouch for me. I gave them confidential information—top secret documents."

"Are you telling me, Lily Dimitrova, that you were a double agent?"

I paused to think about it.

"Yes, I was, of sorts."

"Who were your contacts, exactly?" he asked, as if he hadn't been listening at all.

"I just told you, Dr. Levi, a boy named Peter, and Ioan Goodman."

"Ioan Goodman is dead," the man said. "I know of him. He died trying to kill your boss, Alexander Belev. Unfortunately for you, Ioan cannot vouch for you . . . and a boy named Peter? Seriously? There's thousands of boys named Peter in this country."

As he spoke, I played back the scene on the street below the KEV building. The man who Belev had shot, that must have been Ioan. Peter, young and scared and inexperienced, ran away. I couldn't share this with my interrogator, which made me realize that I couldn't be totally honest. It wouldn't fit with all the KEV and Belev references.

Am I guilty? Do I deserve to be arrested and imprisoned?

"What about Dr. Levi?" I said. "I'm sure you can find him."

"Perhaps," he said. "But it will take time. That is, if he's alive." The interrogator paused, clearly losing his patience. "But you never answered my previous question, Lily?"

"What was that?"

"Do you know where Alexander Belev is located, right now?"

I took a deep breath. I had to decide if I could tell this man the entire truth, or choose which details to share. He'd get them out of me eventually, anyway.

It wasn't that I wanted to protect Belev—not at all. I had already shared his location. But it was a matter of principle. This uncouth interrogator was preparing to rip my life apart, to tear my mind and perhaps my body to shreds. *Why should I go along with this? To comply and appease him?*

They had the record of my employment and employer. My signature and imprints were on at least half of the damning documents in Belev's box, now in their possession. If I gave them Belev's location and they arrested him, would it help or hurt my case? Most importantly, where was any evidence of my assisting Jews in Sofia and the Fatherland Front? *Nowhere*—unless Dr. Levi emerged from the rubble of war unscathed and somehow found his way to this wretched government building.

"Miss Dimitrova?" said my interrogator. "I'm going to ask you one more time. Do you know where we can find Alexander Belev?"

I balked, shaking my head, trying to marshal my thoughts.

The man took his right hand out of his pocket and clicked open a silver switchblade.

PETER

The night I returned home, my father didn't want to speak to me.

I understood why.

Aside from the year and a half of silence, when I arrived in Kyustendil that night, I didn't go directly home.

I spent hours walking the streets with my bag and my pistol, looking for Belev. I wasn't alone. I ran into some old school friends who'd been part of the local underground. They brought me to the partisan headquarters in town—if you could call an old barn a headquarters—and I told them about Belev, his guilty past, his presence in Kyustendil, and his plan to escape. A dozen young guys listened to me intently, though I only knew a few of them.

We split up and scoured the streets and inquired, but nothing came of our night search. I finally went home, deflated.

When I entered through the front door and made my way into the living room, my father scowled at me and went straight to his bedroom. My mother hugged me, cried on my shoulder, and predicted that my dad's mood would change the next morning.

SEPT 10, 1944

PETER

I woke up late.

My dad was at the kitchen table drinking his coffee, reading the newspaper.

His expression hinted at total resentment, but his tone was lukewarm.

"I imagine you drink coffee now?" he said.

"Yeah."

"Come sit down. I'll pour you a cup."

Am I in trouble? Or am I past the point of being in trouble?

Once you've been on your own and at war, it didn't seem possible to go back to being a child—or under the supervision of anyone, for that matter. Of course, there was respect. I always had respect for my father.

He looked at me curiously, set the ceramic cup down, and poured the pure, black, unfiltered coffee. It smelled much better than the crap I'd been drinking for the past year.

"Do you take sugar? Milk? Jesus, I feel like I'm talking to a stranger."

"I'm sorry, Dad," I said without pause.

"I'm just glad you're alive," he said, and let out a long, ragged breath. "Was it what you expected?"

"Not at all," I said.

"Sometimes you have to learn by experience."

His truth was simple and undeniable.

We sipped from our mugs.

"Ioan's dead," I said solemnly.

"I heard."

"I was there. I watched him crumple to the cobble-stones like a sack of potatoes."

"I'm sorry, son."

"The whole thing, I . . ."

My throat clogged up like a blocked spout. I tried to finish my sentence, but I couldn't speak. As I struggled, my father must have instinctively known what was happening inside me because he stood up, came to my side, and gave me a hug.

I burst into tears. I broke down and cried uncontrollably. In that moment, everything that had happened since we'd parted flashed before me. As one sweeping memory, it all seemed like a massive failure. Until my dad spoke to me.

"Peter, I know how it feels to live through a war and be a part of it," he said. "I was about your age during the Great War and tried to get involved. But I wasn't ready for it all—to see death up close. To shoot at people and be shot at. And, later, to wonder what it all meant—if it meant anything. That sort of experience changes a young man. That's why I protested against you staying with the partisans, but I also understand why you wanted to."

I finally detached from my father and gathered the breath to speak. "I didn't even do anything that mattered."

"Yes, you did, son."

I used my sleeve to wipe the tears from my cheeks. "No, I didn't," I insisted.

My dad paused for a while. I noticed there were more gray hairs near his temples than there had been before.

"Do you know what they say here in town about

Dimitar Peshev?" he asked.

"No," I said.

"They say that he's responsible for halting the deportation of Jews, for saving fifty thousand lives."

"But if it weren't for *us*, he wouldn't have known," I said.

"I know."

"And there were so many others who helped, who fought, who risked their lives!"

"I know," my father repeated. "It's what happens in war. Things get foggy. There's only room for a few heroes. The truth gets lost. The reasons for fighting can get lost, too."

Almost in a surreal daze, I nodded in agreement.

"You had reasons, Peter," my dad said, looking out the window toward our neighbor's house. "Every Jew in Kyustendil survived and kept their homes."

"Is David home?" I asked.

"Yes, he is," my dad said. "Go see your best friend. He's been waiting for you to return for over a year."

I hugged my dad again and thanked him. I'd never felt so close to him.

David was still skinny, but had gone from being five centimeters shorter than me to nearly five centimeters taller. *Has that much time passed?* Returning to this life almost didn't seem real.

When he saw me, he smiled and pulled me in for a big hug. He could tell I'd been crying because of my swollen eyes.

"You look like hell," he said.

"It's good to see you, too!"

We went into his house and I greeted his parents and

his little sister. Every interaction I'd had with them before the war had been a polite, routine gesture without any thought or deep care. Now it was different. I hugged them all and would have cried during the reunion if my tears hadn't all been spent on my dad's shoulder.

Just as David's mother offered me tea, their telephone rang. David darted over to pick it up. We could only hear his end of the conversation—brief words of astonishment. He hung up the phone and moved with a sense of urgency.

"Come on, Peter, let's walk to the park," he said. "Radko is there waiting for us."

I knew David was lying, but I got up and said my goodbyes anyway. He'd never liked Radko, nor had I.

When we walked out the front door, he turned right. The park was to the left.

I asked, "Where are we really going?"

"Do you have a gun, Peter?"

"What?" I whispered, stopping short in front of my house.

"Slavcho, a local partisan, is the guy who just called," David said. "He said they found some Nazi guy on his way to the border early this morning. They have him tied up."

Without a word, I ran into my house and straight to my duffel bag, still packed from my journey the previous day. I tossed my clothes and belongings on the bed, but hid my pistol—Ioan's pistol, actually—in a small satchel and threw it over my shoulder. Then I bolted out without explanation and met David across the street, and we nearly sprinted a kilometer to the address near the train station.

Sure, it could have been any old Nazi, but my instincts told me it was Alexander Belev. If there was anyone I wanted to personally remove from the face of the earth, aside from Adolf Hitler himself, it was Belev. Of course, there was the horrendous murder of thousands of Jews. More personally, though, I'd witnessed him kill Ioan, who was like an uncle to me, leaving a widowed family behind. And Belev had tried to *kill me*, too! I could clearly picture him cursing himself for not putting a bullet through my back.

A few blocks from the train station in an undeveloped part of town, two local partisans stood outside of a small abandoned warehouse. Slavcho, David's friend, met us out front and led us into what must have once been the manager's office. The prisoner barely looked in our direction as we entered. Wearing plain clothes, he was tied to the chair he sat on, his head angled down and his wrists bound in the front.

It was Belev.

"Is this the guy you're looking for?" Slavcho asked, exposing his rotten teeth. "He wouldn't tell us his name."

I stepped close and looked him over, making sure he noticed. There was no doubt.

"Yeah, that's Alexander Belev," I said.

"That's not my name," Belev snapped. "I don't know this person."

"We took this from his bag," Slavcho said and handed me identification papers.

"My name's Kyril Botev," Belev said defiantly. "As you can see in my documents."

I held his passport in my hands. *Kyril Botev. Born: NOV-22-1910. Burgas, BG.*

It was fake. I knew it. He knew it.

But I wanted to watch Belev struggle and have my comrades witness it. As the worst kind of traitor, he deserved to be humiliated.

"Mr. Botev," I began, "what is your father's name?"

"Andrey," he said.

"Your mother's?"

"Maria."

"Where were you born?"

He paused. "Varna—I mean, Burgas."

"Nice try," I said and shook my head. "Date of birth?"

"1910."

"The date?" I added.

"November . . . 20," he said.

"Forgot your own birthday, Alexander? I mean, Kyril."

"You piece of shit!" he shouted. "How dare you?"

Slavcho swiftly backhanded Belev, and the impact silenced him immediately. *Was he already breaking?* If so, it was much sooner than I expected. It became obvious that he was a weak man—which must have been why he wanted to feel powerful by sending so many people off to their deaths. I guess his inflated pride couldn't take the indignity of answering to partisan teenagers.

"Well, it's obviously a fake document," David said after looking it over.

"What are we gonna do with him?"

Slavcho glanced at each of us, including the two other guys we'd never met. Not one of us was over the age of twenty, but Slavcho had been a partisan leader in Kyustendil for two years and assumed seniority.

"He needs to be taken to Sofia for a proper trial."

"Proper?" David said. "Rumors are that they're shooting Nazi collaborators by firing squad."

"Whatever the case is, we're not the judge and jury," Slavcho said definitively.

Belev made a groaning noise.

I didn't want to lose this opportunity. *Again.*

I looked at Slavcho. "You're right. We'll escort him. I know Sofia well. I know where to take him. David will help me." I motioned to my old friend.

David shot me an annoyed look for volunteering him without asking.

Slavcho nodded at me, and the two other young partisans stayed mute.

"Okay," he said. "Make sure those cuffs are tight and get him on the next train."

David and I made sure the rope around Belev's wrists was double bound in the front and knotted in such a way that Houdini wouldn't even stand a chance. Then we stood him up and led him out into the street. In normal times, five teenagers leading a handcuffed man down the road in broad daylight might cause a stir, but not after years of war.

Once we crossed the street, Slavcho and his silent henchmen stopped and waved to us.

"Guard him well," Slavcho said.

We rounded the corner, and David gave me a skeptical stare that reminded me he was green. He hadn't been *in* the war at all. But, hell, escorting a prisoner—a former government official—was new to me, too. We walked slowly and kept Belev directly in front of us.

"Why did you volunteer us, Peter?"

"Because I want to see this through," I said.

"What? The war here is over. And you just got back home."

"You don't understand who this man is," I said. "What he did."

At that, Belev halted his stride and turned to me.

"You have no clue who I am or what you're doing, kid."

I was brought up short. I needed to react to any and every movement Belev made. His simple act of stopping made it seem like he was the one in control for the moment.

"Keep walking," I commanded.

We continued walking, though unsteadily. I focused all my attention on Belev. *What is he thinking? Has he accepted defeat, or is he scheming his next move?* As the number of cross streets on the way to the train station dwindled, I kept expecting him to make a break for it, but knew he couldn't get far with his hands bound so tightly. Still, at every corner I readied myself for a quick chase and tackle. *Will he cause a scene and play the victim at the train station? He is an adult and we aren't. What if he convinces others and manages to slip away?*

"How old are you kids?" Belev asked us casually. "Graduated from high school yet?"

I ignored him. So did David.

"Do you really want to go all the way to Sofia?" Belev asked. "Wouldn't you rather make some easy money? Hundreds of dollars, just to be rid of me. I can slip across the border and the new idiotic government in Sofia would never know. They wouldn't even care."

It only took a moment for his words to sink in.

New idiotic government . . . wouldn't even care.

"Wait!" I said, grabbing Belev by the arm and stopping David mid-stride.

I peered down the street toward the train station one block ahead, then to my right down an unpaved road that led into a wood. *What if the new government doesn't care about Belev? Or the evidence against him has been destroyed? Or an old connected friend is able to get him off the hook?* It occurred to me that *anything* could happen once we brought him to the authorities in Sofia. Justice was not guaranteed in this wartime world. Not at all.

"What are you doing, Peter?" David asked.

"Thinking about my good offer," Belev said with a confident smirk on his face.

And it was that grin—that above-the-law, tyrannical expression—which convinced me.

True, Belev, I am thinking. But not at all about your offer.

"Let's go this way," I said, pushing Belev to the right, down the dirt road to nowhere.

"What the hell?" David said.

"We're taking a detour," I said, as we all walked toward the woods.

"Smart," Belev said, self-assured. "Better to complete our transaction out of the public eye."

"You're not taking his offer, are you?" David asked. My best friend looked at me as if he didn't know me anymore.

I didn't say a word.

I pushed Belev forward, prodding him along with my fist. It was already balled up as my anger built—not just for Ioan's death, but for all the Jews whose lives he'd uprooted; the lives he'd stolen so arrogantly. For better or worse, one thing motivated me that morning, plain and simple: revenge.

David shot me a look behind Belev's back. His wide eyes and straight face expressed the unmistakable: *What the hell are we doing?* I returned a knowing glance that I had given him many times growing up, playing sports in the street and war games in the fields: *Trust me.*

We'd made it off the road and well into the dense growth of trees when Belev, in front of us, stopped on his own, as if he were in charge.

"This is more than sufficient," he told us.

"You're right," I said.

"Hand me my bag," Belev said to David, who held it over his shoulder.

David didn't hand it over politely, but threw it on the ground in front of him, glad to offload the weight. Belev raised his hands to remind us his wrists were bound.

"I'll need this restraint taken off if we are to conduct business," he said. "I have the cash for you in my bag."

David hesitated. "Are we doing this?" he asked me.

I gave him the look again: *Trust me.*

"Careful," I said to David, then to Belev. "No sudden movements."

As David used his pocket knife to cut Belev's hands free, I reached into my satchel and pulled out my pistol.

Both David and our prisoner immediately locked their eyes on the gun.

For a few seconds, there was no sound between us but the humming cicadas.

"Alexander Belev," I said, my voice shaky and echoing in my ears, as if they were not attached to my head, "get on your knees and hold your hands up."

"I beg your pardon?" he said, in shock. "This is no way to negotiate."

"I'm not negotiating," I said. "I don't want your money."

Belev paused in shock, then laughed in disbelief as if he still held the cards.

"You're making a big mistake," he said. "The war's not over, you know. I have very important friends in Germany."

"Germans?" I said, waving the gun in Belev's direction. "I don't see any of your Nazi friends here."

"Are you crazy?" David blurted out.

I kept my eyes locked on Belev. "David," I said, "you have no idea what this man has done."

Belev was now on his knees, his bag within arm's reach. It wasn't until that moment that I realized we'd been too preoccupied to check his bag beforehand. *Stupid, amateur partisans.* That's what Belev was counting on—capitalizing on our youth and inexperience.

"A-are you going to kill him?" David stammered.

"No, of course not," Belev interjected. "You're not even certain of my identity. You wouldn't want to kill an innocent man."

"Innocent?" I said, never looking away from Belev's hands and the bag in front of him. "My best friend here, David, is Jewish." My voice was steadier now. I was still focused on Belev, my gun pointed at the ground somewhere between his knees. "You would've had him and his family sent to a death camp in Poland if you'd had the choice."

I raised my pistol, straightened my right arm tight, and pointed the barrel at Belev's chest.

"That's not true," Belev blurted.

"He's lying," I said to David, keeping my eyes on Belev.

"Peter, what if he's not lying?"

"He's lying," I said confidently.

"I can do more than pay you!" Belev pleaded, his smug tone gone—finally replaced by fear. "I have connections. I'll get you anything you want!"

"Anything?" I asked.

"Yes," Belev affirmed.

"Can you bring back my friend, Ioan?"

"Who?" he asked.

"That man you shot and killed on Dundukov Street in front of your office building?"

Belev tilted his head in thought, as if he had to make an effort to recall exactly who he'd murdered.

"Oh, the failed assassin?" Belev asked. "Wait . . . were you there?"

"Yes, I was," I said calmly, stoically focused. "You killed my friend and shot at my back as I ran down the street."

"Ah, that's what this is all about? That's why you want to kill me?"

"No," I said. "I'm going to kill you because you murdered over ten thousand Jews and you tried to kill fifty thousand more. You evicted families. You ruined lives and almost this entire nation."

Belev laughed like a crazed man. "You actually think that saving all those Jews would make Bulgaria better off?"

"I'm sure of one thing," I replied. "That the world will be better off without *you*."

"Stop this childish game," he snapped, "and take me

back to Sofia, you idiot!"

"Wait!" David yelled.

I turned my eyes toward my best friend for a split second.

Belev lunged straight for his bag.

I aimed and shot at him twice. *Pop! Pop!* Like firecrackers. One bullet hit his shoulder, the other punctured his chest. Belev's body leapt back and fell limp to the ground. I watched the man crumple. Lifeless. I stared, frozen in a surreal haze, as his dark blood pooled on the dirt.

Near panic, David could barely catch his breath.

I held myself together the best that I could.

David and I walked back toward our neighborhood, taking the long way so we could plan what to do next. At first it was difficult to speak, but we managed.

Less than an hour later, I returned to the dead body alone with a spare can of gasoline taken from my garage. I poured it all over Belev, lit a match, and cremated him.

Justice the old-fashioned way, I thought.

There would be no trial in Sofia.

And, with retribution against Nazi collaborators common in those last months of 1944, there would be no trial for me, either.

The leader of the Nazi department officially tasked with exterminating Jews in Bulgaria was dead.

My war was officially over.

LILY

I eventually told my interrogator the truth.

I told him that Belev would be trying to escape into Macedonia through Kyustendil. That I worked for the KEV only to support my poor parents in Stara Zagora. That I didn't have political preferences—not before, during the war, or now. That I began leaking information to Dr. Levi and others after I witnessed the horrendous deportation of Jews in Skopje.

I even told him that I had slept with Belev in order to save myself from his suspicion.

It didn't matter.

None of it mattered.

The man who questioned me was an idiot who must have thought that every word that came out of my mouth was a lie to protect myself, or some half-truth to deflect responsibility.

He repeated, "Who can trust a double agent? They lie to everyone!"

It made me wonder why he even bothered asking me any questions in the first place, if nothing I said could be trusted or proven beyond my word.

When I gave him the truth and he didn't believe me the first time, he slapped my left cheek, hard—so hard, it hurt my neck on top of the burning sting.

Ironically, he didn't actually use his silver knife until I had already answered all his questions truthfully. There was something about the idea of me helping the Fatherland Front *and* being fine with outing Belev's current escape plans that set him off. But who knows?

When I tried to tell him the truth and he didn't believe me the second time, he grabbed my ear, pressed the knife point into the middle of it, and swiped up hard and fast. I screamed like a wounded animal. It felt like half my ear had been sliced open. Blood poured into my ear duct and off the lobe onto my neck and shoulder. I wailed. I whimpered. I thought that it might stop there, but it just got worse.

He repeated questions and I repeated my honest answers.

No matter what, he didn't believe me and went back to his macabre ear fetish. In those long moments of pain and bloody misery, I thought it would never end.

After an hour of torture, I would swear that he simply hated women, characterized them all as lying cheaters, and was taking it all out on me.

This vile, sadistic man sliced through my left ear three times, and my right ear twice. I lost so much blood that I became light-headed and fainted more than once. By the time my interrogator left the room, my entire blouse was dark red and I must have looked like some house of horrors freak show. I was semi-conscious when two men walked in, cleaned me up a bit, and wrapped my head with a bandage that covered both ears tightly. It hurt so much I would have screamed if I'd had any energy left. But all that came out of me was a miserable, guttural moan.

The two men dragged me back to my bare cell.

The only thing inside was a bucket to piss and shit in.

SEPT 11, 1944

LILY

One of the guards was actually nice to me this morning.

The young man entered and placed my ration of bread, water, and two slices of *lukanka* next to the door. Minutes later, he returned with a newspaper and a very small pencil. I assumed they didn't give prisoners normal-sized pencils for fear that they might try to commit suicide with it. I can't say that it didn't cross my mind.

Death would be freedom at this point.

I read the news about the Soviet army arriving in Sofia. Liberating us from the Nazis. I read about the rebuilding efforts in the streets being on hold until the new government convened. I read about the so-called People's Courts and firing squads for Nazi collaborators.

Apparently, they were still searching for former pro-Nazi officials.

Had they found Belev? Or had he escaped? Was he alive or dead? Did I care either way?

After reading the news, I started to use the margins to write. To try and make sense of my predicament, I suppose. I started from the beginning—when my consciousness awoke and I began to see this whole war and my role in it differently. Shamefully.

The train station in Skopje.

I wrote in the smallest spaces imaginable, until there was no half centimeter free on those pages. When the same young guard returned with a bowl of soup for lunch, I thanked him for the newspaper and pencil.

"You're welcome," he said, his head tilted away as if he were ashamed to look at me.

"Are they going to kill me?" I asked.

"I don't know, Miss." He backed his way toward the cell door.

"Can I ask you for any blank paper?" I said meekly.

He looked me in the eyes for once and must have seen the definition of pathetic: a tortured prisoner with no hope, covered in her own dried blood, perhaps wanting to write her last will and testament.

"I'll try," he said, and left.

About an hour later, the young guard returned with a thin notebook. Instead of throwing it into my cell like I was an animal, he handed it to me through the bars. It was a supremely humane act.

"Thank you," I said, my voice a shell of its normal self.

"Thank my friend, Miss," he said. "His name's Peter."

I didn't understand. I didn't know what to say.

"What's your name?" I asked.

"Max," he said and left the room.

The notebook—that unlikely gift—stared back at me.

I have been writing in it ever since.

I have been writing in it for you, reader, so that if Dr. Levi never emerges to testify on my behalf and I am killed by a callous new communist government or a "People's Court" for my association with the KEV, then at least someone will know the truth. At least someone will understand what I did. What I tried to do. And will know that I am not perfect. That nobody is, but that we do what we can under the circumstances.

Ultimately, *you* will be the judge, not these ruffians. But hopefully, in doing so, you will put yourself in my shoes.

There's the right side and the wrong side. Sometimes it's difficult to know which is which, but when you do recognize right from wrong, hopefully—for you—it's not too late. Because you can't be on both sides at the same time. It doesn't work like that.

I fear it's too late for me.

They will torture me over and over until they realize that maybe I am telling the truth after all—and that maybe I'm not such a bad person. And they will let me go. *But where can I go now?*

Or maybe they will simply kill me when they get tired of hearing the same old honest answers.

I don't know. I don't know much at all anymore, and I'm scared to death.

They say that people's minds are more likely to be lost during the fog of war. But now that it's over for Bulgaria, I wonder if the fog of post-war will be even worse. If something more will be lost.

Something more than my own life.

AFTERWORD
A Historical Note

Most of the events depicted in this novel are based on actual history. Though the story is not told in perfect chronological order, most of the main events and key sequences are chronological and historical. Creative license has been used liberally in the imagined details and scenes in order to fit the plotline, serve the story, and develop the main characters. However, the author was inspired by real historical events and individuals, and attempted to be true to the historical context throughout.

Some of the characters are based on real people. Though Misho and Peter are entirely fictionalized characters, they were imagined in a real context and connected to real people—namely Archbishop (Metropolitan) Stefan, Rabbi Daniel Zion, Dimitar Peshev, and the delegation that went to Sofia to defend the Jews of Kyustendil. For instance, Metropolitan Stefan was steadfastly and publicly opposed to discrimination against Bulgarian Jews and had some degree of influence on King Boris—who did much to obstruct Jewish deportations and met directly with Adolf Hitler several times during the course of the war. King Boris did die mysteriously only days after his final visit with Hitler. Rabbi Daniel Zion was, in fact, given refuge by Archbishop Stefan for a time, participated in the May protests, and was imprisoned in a Bulgarian concentration camp until the end of the war. However, his personal interactions—as well as all dialogue in this novel—has been fictionalized. Indeed, Dimitar Peshev protested against the deportation plans on March 9, and organized a petition in Parliament to end discrimination against all Jewish citizens. His anti-Nazi efforts were clearly influential, and are remembered by the Jewish community in Bulgaria and beyond. There is a museum in Kyustendil dedicated to him for his crucial role in saving the country's Jewish population, though it was largely covered up during the communist era (1945–1990), when credit was given only to the communist partisans in the Fatherland Front.

The fictionalized character Lily Dimitrova is based on Lily Panitza, a real young woman who worked for Alexander Belev and the pro-Nazi "Commissariat for Jewish Questions" (KEV) during World War II. According to the records, on multiple occasions she risked her job and safety to inform Jewish leaders in Sofia about the government's plans for arresting and deporting the nation's Jews. Her behind-the-scenes work and strategic information leaks certainly had an impact in alerting the Jewish community and those with influence. Paradoxically, Lily Panitza reportedly had a love affair with Belev sometime during the war. Knowing her general actions but not the specifics, the author fictionalized all dialogue and story details concerning the character of Lily.

German pressure to deport Jews dissipated after September of 1943, and the Allied bombing of Bulgaria began soon after. The war essentially ended for Bulgaria in early September 1944, when Soviet forces liberated the nation from the Nazis. Because of Lily Panitza's affiliation with the pro-German government—like many federal officials and employees who had supported Nazism/fascism—she was arrested and tortured. Her life was spared (though she died soon after release), but the lives of many former government officials were not. Peshev was sentenced to imprisonment for a time. Gabrovski was executed. Alexander Belev, fearing for his life, did actually try to escape. Before reaching the Macedonian border, he was caught and identified outside of Kyustendil by a group of Jewish men. One of those young men (whose identity is unknown) took Belev away from the others and shot him in the head.

ACKNOWLEDGMENTS

Writing this novel started decades ago with a love of history, and was accelerated by a move to a country about which I knew nothing. Thank you to the countless people between Sofia, Bulgaria, and San Diego, California, who have piqued my curiosity on this topic and added layers to my interest and knowledge. Special thanks to Jennifer Silva-Redmond for her professional editing advice and support. Additional thanks to three former high school students who spent hours reading and revising this story: Gergana Papazova, Chiara Margetides, and Gerald "Trey" Whitfield—your contributions certainly added to its authenticity. I extend my gratitude to Jeffrey Goldman for believing in this manuscript and Kate Murray for her editing input. Lastly, a general thank you to all of my friends and family for their love and support—past and present.